Safeguarded By The First Sergeant

The Brotherhood, Volume 4

Mia Caldwell and Mylia Ashton

Published by Mia Caldwell, 2024.

Blurb

A past they can't outrun, and a fight they can't afford to lose.
WHEN A ROUTINE FLIGHT puts pilot Kat Deacon face-to-face with a deadly human trafficking ring, her past collides with a ruthless present. Now hiding at a fortified ranch with her ex-husband and former soldier, Mike Deacon, Kat is thrust into a high-stakes fight against Los Coyotes, a brutal gang with cartel ties smuggling people across the U.S.-Mexico border.

With the traffickers closing in, Mike and his brotherhood of battle-hardened allies, along with their wives, must hold the line. As old wounds reopen, and sparks fly between Kat and Mike, survival becomes more than just defeating the enemy. It's about reclaiming what they've lost and staying alive long enough to do so. The love never died, but the past still hangs between them, and she has to know why he turned from her back then if they can ever move forward.

Outnumbered and outgunned, can they outlast the siege? Or will the darkness of their pasts consume them all?

Chapter 1—Kat

KAT DEACON SQUINTED against the harsh Texas sun as she guided her Pilatus P-12 across the cloudless sky. The familiar hum of the engines provided a soothing backdrop to her thoughts as she approached the border between Texas and Mexico.

"Just another routine charter flight," she muttered to herself, adjusting her course slightly to account for a mild crosswind.

As she neared her destination, movement on the ground caught her attention. Kat lowered her altitude for a better view, curiosity piqued by the unusual activity in such a remote area. "What the hell?"

A group of people huddled together near a small cluster of vehicles. Even from this height, the tension was intense. Kat's stomach tightened as she recognized the telltale signs of a confrontation unfolding.

She reached for her radio, hesitating for a moment before deciding against calling it in. Without concrete evidence, it could be nothing more than a simple disagreement. Still, something about the scene below set her nerves on edge.

Kat circled back around, flying lower this time. The details came into sharper focus—a mix of men, women, and even children stood together, their body language radiating fear. Facing them was a smaller group, their stance aggressive and threatening.

"Oh, no," Kat whispered as she saw the glint of metal in the sunlight. Guns.

Before she could fully process what was happening, muzzle flashes erupted from the smaller group. The horrifying scene played out in slow motion as bodies crumpled to the ground.

Her hands shook on the controls as she fought the urge to vomit. She'd just witnessed a massacre.

"Fuck, fuck, fuck," she chanted, her mind racing. Should she report it? What if they saw her? What if they came after her?

A flash of movement caught her attention. One of the victims was still alive, crawling away from the carnage. Without thinking, Kat banked hard, searching for a place to land.

"This is insane," she murmured, spotting a stretch of flat land not far from the scene. "What the hell am I doing?"

Her father's voice echoed in her head. *Sometimes, baby girl, you gotta do what's right, even when it's hard.*

She took a deep breath, fortifying herself for what was to come. As she brought the plane down for a rough landing, she prayed she wasn't making a terrible mistake. The moment the wheels touched down, she killed the engines and scrambled out of the cockpit. The oppressive heat hit her like a wall as she sprinted toward the lone survivor.

"Hey," she called out, her voice cracking. "I'm here to help."

The figure—a young woman—looked up at Kat with wild, terrified eyes. Blood stained her clothes, and she clutched her side in pain.

Kat reached the woman's side, kneeling down beside her. "Can you walk? We need to get out of here fast."

The woman nodded weakly, allowing Kat to help her to her feet. They stumbled toward the plane, the woman's labored breathing filling the eerie silence.

A shout in the distance made Kat's blood run cold. They'd been spotted.

"Shit," she said softly, practically dragging the injured woman the last few yards to the plane. "Come on, we're almost there."

As they reached the aircraft, the sound of engines revving in the distance spurred Kat into action. She helped the woman into the cabin before sprinting to the cockpit. Her hands flew over the controls, muscle memory taking over as she started the pre-flight sequence. The familiar whine of the engines starting up provided a small measure of comfort.

She glanced over her shoulder at her unexpected passenger. The woman had slumped against the seat, her eyes closed.

"Hey," Kat called out. "Stay with me, okay? What's your name?"

The woman's eyes fluttered open. "Maria."

"Okay, Maria. I'm Kat. We're getting out of here, all right? Just hang on."

As she turned back to the controls, a bullet pinged off the fuselage. With a curse, she pushed the throttle forward, the plane lurching into motion. Another shot rang out, missing the windshield by inches.

Her heart hammered as she guided the plane down the makeshift runway. The uneven ground jostled them violently, but she kept her focus on getting airborne. "Come on, baby," she urged the plane. "Don't fail me now." She urged the plane faster, desperate to escape the hail of gunfire behind her. The engines roared, straining against the uneven terrain. Just as the nose lifted, a sickening thud reverberated through the fuselage. The controls jerked in her hands.

"No, no, no," she muttered, fighting to maintain control.

The ground fell away, but the plane listed dangerously to one side. Smoke poured from the right engine. Kat's gaze darted between her instruments and the rapidly approaching tree line.

"Mayday, mayday," she called into her radio. "This is November-Three-Four-Seven-Kilo-Delta. I've been shot down and am going down near..." She rattled off her last known coordinates before the radio crackled and went dead.

Kat glanced back at Maria, who stared at her with wide, terrified eyes. "Hang on. This is gonna be rough."

The treetops rushed up to meet them. She yanked back on the yoke, desperately trying to level out. Branches scraped the underside of the plane with a horrific screech. The right wing caught, spinning them violently.

Everything blurred into a sickening whirl of motion. The deafening crunch of metal filled her ears as they slammed into the ground. Her head snapped forward, then back against the seat. Pain exploded behind her eyes as darkness consumed her.

KAT REGAINED CONSCIOUSNESS slowly, her head throbbing. The acrid smell of smoke and fuel filled her nostrils. She blinked, trying to focus. The cockpit was a mangled mess of twisted metal and shattered glass.

"Maria," she croaked, twisting to look behind her. The woman lay slumped in her seat, blood trickling from a gash on her forehead.

She fumbled with her seatbelt, her fingers clumsy and uncooperative. Finally free, she climbed out of her seat, wincing as pain shot through her ribs. She stumbled to Maria's side.

"Hey, wake up," said Kat, gently shaking the woman's shoulder. "We need to get out of here."

Her eyes fluttered open. She groaned, looking around in confusion.

"Come on. Can you move?"

Maria nodded weakly. Kat helped her out of the seat, supporting most of her weight as they made their way to the emergency exit. The door was jammed, but she managed to force it open with a few solid kicks.

They tumbled out onto the forest floor. Kat half-carried, half-dragged Maria away from the wreckage. They collapsed against a large oak tree, both panting heavily.

"Are you okay?" asked Kat, examining Maria for obvious injuries.

"I think so," said Maria, her voice shaky. "My side hurts, but I don't think it's too bad." Her English was a bit broken, but that could have been from her injury more than her knowledge of the language.

She nodded, relieved as she surveyed their surroundings, trying to get her bearings. Dense forest stretched in every direction. The late afternoon sun filtered through the leaves but did little to help her orient.

"We need to keep moving," said Kat. "Those men will be looking for us."

Maria's dark eyes widened in fear. "They will kill us if they find us."

"I know," she said grimly. "That's why we can't stay here. Can you walk?"

The other woman nodded, struggling to her feet with her help. They set off deeper into the forest, moving as quickly as Maria's injuries would allow. Kat tried to formulate a plan.

"There has to be a town or a road nearby. If we can just find some people, we'll be safe."

As they pushed through the underbrush, her thoughts turned to the horror she had witnessed. "What happened back there? Who were those men?"

Maria's face crumpled. "They are monsters. We thought they would help us cross the border to find work. Instead, they murdered everyone." She choked back a sob. "My husband, my little boy...gone."

Kat's heart ached for the woman. She knew something about losing a husband, those hers wasn't dead. He was just lost to her. "I am so sorry," she said softly. "We'll make sure they pay for what they've done."

A twig snapped behind them. Kat whirled around, her body tensing. "Did you hear that?" she whispered.

Maria nodded, her eyes wide with fear.

They stood frozen, listening intently. The forest had gone eerily quiet. Then, a man's voice cut through the stillness.

"I saw smoke this way. The plane must have gone down nearby."

She grabbed Maria's hand. "Run."

They crashed through the underbrush, branches whipping at their faces. Her lungs burned as she pushed herself to keep going. The sound of pursuit grew closer.

"There. I see them."

A bullet whizzed past Kat's ear. She ducked instinctively, pulling Maria down with her. They scrambled behind a fallen log, hearts pounding.

"What do we do?" whispered Maria, trembling.

Kat scanned their surroundings desperately. She saw a small opening in the hillside nearby. "There. I think it's a cave. If we can make it there, we might be able to lose them."

Maria nodded. Kat counted to three, then they sprinted for the cave entrance. More gunshots rang out, but they made it inside unscathed.

The cave was dark and damp. She led Maria deeper inside, feeling their way along the rough stone walls. After what seemed like an eternity, the sounds of pursuit faded. They slumped to the ground, exhausted. She strained her ears, listening for any sign of danger. All she could hear was their ragged breathing and the steady drip of water echoing through the cave. "I think we lost them," Kat whispered. "For now, at least."

Maria nodded, tears streaming down her face. "Thank you," she said softly. "You saved my life."

Kat squeezed her hand. "We're not out of this yet, but I promise, I'll do everything I can to get us both to safety." As the adrenaline faded, the pain from her own injuries made itself known. She winced, gingerly probing her ribs. Definitely bruised and possibly cracked. Her head throbbed, and she could feel dried blood on her temple.

"Are you hurt badly?" asked Maria, concern evident in her voice.

Kat shook her head. "Nothing too serious. How about you? How is your side?"

Maria lifted her shirt, revealing an angry bruise spreading across her ribcage. "It hurts to breathe deeply, but I don't think anything is broken."

Kat nodded. "Good. We need to rest for a bit, but we can't stay here long. Those men won't give up easily."

They sat in silence for a while, each lost in their own thoughts. They needed food, water, and medical supplies. More importantly, they needed to contact the authorities.

"Maria," said Kat softly. "I need you to tell me everything you know about those men. Who they are and where they operate from. Anything that might help us."

Maria took a shaky breath. "They call themselves Los Coyotes. They promise to help people cross the border and find work in America, but it's all lies." Her voice broke. "They take your money, then kill you and steal everything you have."

Kat's blood boiled at the cruelty. "How long have they been operating?"

"I don't know for certain," said Maria. "But I have heard stories for years. No one ever does anything because they are too powerful, too well-connected, and people like me and Juan keep them in business with our desperation to have a new life. If only I'd listened to the whispered warnings. Miguel..." She dissolved into sobs.

Kat patted her shoulder, assuming Miguel was her little boy, who was now dead. "We're going to make sure they're stopped."

Maria looked at her with skepticism. "How? They will kill us if they find us."

"They won't find us," said Kat firmly. "And we are not going to hide forever. We're going to fight back."

She stood, wincing slightly at the movement. "Come on. We need to keep moving. There has to be a town nearby where we can get help."

As they made their way deeper into the cave, searching for another exit, she analyzed the situation. She had seen too much to walk away now. The cave narrowed, forcing them to squeeze through tight passages. Her claustrophobia threatened to overwhelm her, but she pushed it down. They had no choice but to keep going.

After what felt like hours, a faint glimmer of light appeared ahead. She inhaled raggedly before saying, "Look. I think I see a way out."

They emerged from the cave into a small clearing. The sun was setting. Kat took a deep breath, savoring the fresh air.

"Which way should we go?" asked Maria, looking around uncertainly.

Kat scanned their surroundings, trying to get her bearings. In the distance, she spotted a faint plume of smoke rising above the trees.

"There," she said, pointing. "That has to be a house or a camp. It's our best chance of finding help."

They set off toward the smoke, moving as quickly and quietly as possible through the dense underbrush. As they walked, her mind churned with questions. "How did you end up with Los Coyotes? If you don't mind me asking."

Maria was quiet for a long moment before responding. "My husband and I...we wanted a better life for our son. Things were so hard in our village. No work and no future." She wiped away a tear. "We saved for years to pay the coyotes. We thought they would help us start a new life in America."

Kat's heart ached for the woman. "I am so sorry," she said. "What they did to you and your family... it's unforgivable."

Maria nodded, her eyes filled with grief but also determination. "That is why we must stop them. So no one else suffers like this."

As they pushed through a particularly dense patch of brush, she suddenly froze. She held up a hand, signaling Maria to stop. "Do you hear that?" she whispered.

In the distance, they could hear the faint sound of voices and laughter. Kat's heart raced with hope and fear. It could be help.. or it could be Los Coyotes. "We need to be careful," said Kat. "Stay low and quiet. We'll get closer and see who it is before we show ourselves."

They crept forward, using the fading light and dense foliage for cover. As they neared the source of the voices, she caught a glimpse of a small cabin through the trees. A group of men sat around a campfire, drinking and talking loudly.

Her blood ran cold as she recognized one of the men from the massacre. These weren't potential rescuers. They had stumbled upon a Los Coyotes hideout.

She turned to Maria, putting a finger to her lips. They needed to get out of there, fast, but as they started to back away, her foot caught on a root. She stumbled, catching herself just before she fell.

The snap of a twig under her foot seemed to echo through the forest.

One of the men at the campfire stood up, peering into the darkness. *"¿Escuchaste eso?"* She knew enough Spanish to know he'd said, *"Did you hear that?"*

She grabbed Maria's hand. They had to run, now, but which way? In the growing darkness, it was impossible to tell which direction led to safety and which led back to their pursuers.

As footsteps approached their hiding spot, she made a split-second decision. She pulled Maria in the opposite direction, praying it was the right choice. They crashed through the underbrush without worrying about stealth. Behind them, shouts of alarm rang out. The hunt was on once again.

Her lungs burned, and her ribs ached, as she pushed herself to keep going. She glanced back at Maria, who stumbled along behind her, clutching her injured side.

"Come on. We can't let them catch us."

They plunged deeper into the forest, the sounds of pursuit growing closer. Kat's mind raced, searching for a way out of this nightmare. If they could just find somewhere to hide, maybe they could lose their pursuers in the darkness.

A gunshot cracked through the air. Maria cried out and fell to the ground. She skidded to a stop, mouth dry. "Maria." She rushed to the woman's side, horrified to see blood spreading across her shirt. "No, no, no. Come on, we have to keep moving."

Maria's eyes were wide with pain and fear. "I can't," she whispered. "Go. Save yourself."

"I'm not leaving you," she insisted, trying to help Maria to her feet, but the woman's legs buckled, unable to support her weight.

Another shot rang out, closer this time. She looked up to see shadowy figures moving through the trees. They were out of time.

"I'm sorry." Maria gasped. "Thank you for trying to help me, but I'd rather be with Juan and Miguel anyway. Bless me, Father..." Her eyes fluttered closed.

Her throat tightened with grief and rage. She wanted to stay and fight, to make these monsters pay for what they'd done, but she stood no chance against them.

With a last anguished look at Maria's still form, she forced herself to her feet and ran. Branches tore at her clothes and skin as she plunged blindly through the forest. She had no idea where she was going—only that she had to get away.

A bullet whizzed past her ear. Kat ducked instinctively, losing her footing on the uneven ground. She tumbled down a steep incline, rolling over rocks and roots. Pain exploded through her body as something slammed into her shoulder.

She came to a stop at the bottom of a ravine, dazed and disoriented. Her left arm hung uselessly at her side, and she tasted blood in her mouth. Footsteps and voices approached from above.

Fighting down waves of nausea, she dragged herself to her feet. She stumbled forward, using the ravine walls for support. Her shoulder throbbed with each movement, but she forced herself to keep going.

The sound of running water reached her ears. She pushed through a tangle of bushes to find herself on the bank of a swift-moving stream. Without hesitation, she waded in, gasping at the icy shock.

The current tugged at her legs as she made her way across. On the far bank, she paused to catch her breath. Her fingers brushed something in her pocket—her phone. By some miracle, it had survived the fall.

Kat pulled it out with trembling hands. The screen was cracked, but it still worked. She had no signal, but at least she had a lifeline. If she could just find her way to civilization, she might have a chance.

Gritting her teeth against the pain, she pushed herself upright. She couldn't let Maria's sacrifice be in vain. Somehow, she would survive this, and she would make sure Los Coyotes paid for their crimes.

As she limped into the darkness, Kat's determination grew. She might be injured and alone, but she wasn't defeated. Not yet.

Chapter 2—Mike

MIKE DEACON'S PHONE buzzed insistently, jarring him from his conversation with Cooper. He glanced at the screen, his eyebrows shooting up when he saw Kat's name flashing. "Kat?" he answered, instinctive tension creeping into his voice. He was always on guard when speaking to his ex-wife, lest he say too much.

"Mike..." Kat's voice was weak. "I need help."

He stiffened, every muscle coiling with sudden alertness. "What happened? Where are you?"

"Attacked... near the border..." Kat's words slurred together, punctuated by ragged breaths. "Saw something... they're after me..."

"Hold on, Kat. Stay with me," he urged. He caught Cooper's eye, mouthing 'emergency' as he moved.

Cooper nodded, immediately understanding. He began assembling supplies while Mike focused on keeping Kat talking.

"Can you give me any landmarks? Anything to help us find you?" he asked, his voice steady despite the fear gripping his chest.

"Trees... a stream..." Kat's voice faded, then returned. "Old barn... red paint..."

Mike relayed the information to Cooper, who was already pulling up satellite imagery on his tablet.

"We're coming for you, Kat. Just hold on," he said, though his throat was tight with worry.

"Mike..." Kat's voice was barely a whisper now. "I'm sorry... for everything..."

"No, don't do that. You're going to be fine," he said through a lump in his throat. "Keep talking to me, Kat."

But there was only silence on the other end.

"Kat? Kat." Mike's voice rose, panic edging in. He turned to Cooper urgently. "We need to move. Now."

Cooper nodded, already heading for the door. "I've got a rough location. Let's go."

Mike followed, his mind racing. As they stepped outside, he saw Viper and Sawyer already loading up the truck, alerted by Cooper's quick text. Fortunately, Sawyer and Kinsey owned a ranch nearby, and Viper and Sage's property edged Cooper and Nina's. It was like one big pain-in-the-ass family for which he was grateful, especially in times like these.

"What's the situation?" asked Viper, his single eye fixed on Mike. The patch covering the missing one was in place.

"Kat's in trouble. Attacked near the border. She's hurt badly," he said tersely, climbing into the passenger seat.

Sawyer whistled low. "Your ex-wife? Damn, brother. We'll find her."

As Cooper gunned the engine, Mike's thoughts whirled. He and Kat had divorced years ago, pushed apart by his PTSD and injuries, but his love for her had never truly died. Now, faced with the possibility of losing her forever, he couldn't deny how much she still meant to him.

The truck roared down the dusty Texas roads, eating up miles as they raced against time. His hand hovered over his phone, willing it to ring again and praying to hear Kat's voice once more.

"Talk to me, Coop," said Mike. "What are we looking at?"

Cooper's gaze remained fixed on the road as he spoke. "Based on what said Kat and the satellite imagery, I've got a rough area pinpointed. It's about fifty miles south, near an old logging road that crosses into Mexico."

Viper leaned forward from the backseat. "Any idea who might be after her?"

Mike shook his head, frustration etched on his face. "No clue. Kat ferries people and cargo in that jet her dad left her."

"The one she flew us in to Chicago?" asked Viper.

"Yeah. She goes into some remote areas. Maybe she saw something she wasn't supposed to."

"Could be cartel activity," said Sawyer grimly. "That area's known for smuggling."

The implications hung heavy in the air. If the cartels were involved, this was even more dangerous than they'd initially thought.

"We'll need to be careful," said Cooper. "We can't go in guns blazing without knowing the full situation."

He nodded, though every fiber of his being screamed to rush in and find Kat. "Agreed. We'll do recon first, then extract her as quickly and quietly as possible."

As they drove, his mind wandered back to happier times with Kat. Their wedding day, and her radiant smile as she walked down the aisle. Lazy Sunday mornings spent in bed, laughing and talking about their dreams for the future. The pride in her eyes when he returned from his first deployment.

Then came the IED that changed everything. The nightmares, the pain, and the anger that pushed her away. His fear of hurting her had led him to go before he could. Mike closed his eyes, regret washing over him. He'd thought he was protecting her by leaving, sparing her from the broken man he'd become. Now, he realized how wrong he'd been, and how much time they'd lost.

"We're getting close," said Cooper, snapping Mike back to the present. "There's the old barn Kat mentioned."

Mike leaned forward, scanning the landscape. The red barn stood out against the scrubby terrain, its paint faded and peeling. Beyond it, a dense copse of trees marked the location of the stream she had described.

"Pull over here," he said. "We'll go the rest of the way on foot."

Cooper eased the truck off the road, concealing it behind a rocky outcropping. The men quickly geared up, checking weapons and comms.

"We don't know what we're walking into," said Mike as they prepared to move out. "Stay alert and watch each other's backs."

The others nodded. This wasn't just a rescue mission. It was personal. Kat was family, even if she and Mike were no longer together.

As they moved silently through the underbrush, his heart beat erratically. Every rustle of leaves and snapping twig set his nerves on edge. She was out here somewhere, hurt and alone. He had to find her.

"Movement ahead," whispered Viper, gesturing with his rifle.

Mike dropped into a crouch, peering through the foliage. He held his breath as he spotted a figure stumbling through the trees.

"Kat." He recognized her instantly despite the distance and her disheveled state.

Without hesitation, Mike broke cover, racing toward her. "Kat. It's Mike. We're here."

She turned at the sound of his voice, her eyes wide with relief and fear. She took a step toward him, then collapsed. He reached her just as she fell, catching her in his arms. "I've got you," he murmured, cradling her against his chest. "You're safe now."

Her eyes fluttered open, unfocused and hazy with pain. "Mike? You came..."

"Of course, I came," said Mike, his voice thick with emotion. "I'll always come for you, Kat. You came through for me when Viper needed help. It's what we do." There was so much more to it, and more he wanted to say, but this wasn't the time.

The others quickly surrounded them, providing cover as he assessed her injuries. She was battered and bruised, with a nasty gash on her arm that was still oozing blood, and her shoulder was either dislocated or broken.

"We need to move," said Cooper as he scanned the tree line. "Whoever was after her might still be out there."

He nodded, carefully lifting Kat into his arms. She whimpered softly at the movement, her head lolling against his shoulder. "Stay with me, Kat," he pleaded as they began making their way back to the truck. "Just hold on a little longer."

He cradled Kat's limp form, racing back toward the truck. The dense foliage whipped at his face and arms, but he barely noticed, focused solely on getting her to safety. Cooper led the way, his rifle at the ready, while Viper and Sawyer brought up the rear, scanning for threats.

They were mere yards from the vehicle when the first gunshot cracked through the air. Mike instinctively ducked, shielding Kat with his body as he dove behind a large boulder.

"At least six," shouted Viper, returning fire. "I see tatts that suggest...cartel?"

Mike's mind raced. They were pinned down, outgunned, and Kat needed medical attention fast. He glanced at Cooper, who had taken cover behind a nearby tree. "We need to get to the truck," he yelled over the gunfire.

Cooper nodded. "I'll lay down cover fire. You make a run for it with Kat. Viper, Sawyer, you're on me."

Mike tightened his grip on her, preparing to move. Her eyes fluttered open, unfocused and glazed with pain. "Mike?" she mumbled.

"I've got you," he assured her, his voice low and urgent. "Just hold on."

Cooper raised three fingers, counting down. As his last finger dropped, he and the others opened fire, unleashing a barrage that momentarily pushed back the cartel soldiers.

Mike seized the opportunity, sprinting toward the truck with Kat in his arms. Bullets whizzed past, kicking up dirt at his feet. His lungs burned, muscles screaming in protest, but he pushed on.

He reached the truck, yanking open the rear door and carefully laying Kat across the back seat. As he climbed in beside her, a searing pain tore through his left arm. He gritted his teeth, ignoring the blood now soaking his sleeve.

"Go," he shouted to Cooper, who had just slid behind the wheel.

The engine roared to life as Viper and Sawyer piled into the bed of the truck, still returning fire. Cooper floored the accelerator, tires spinning in the loose dirt before finding purchase.

As they sped away, Mike turned his attention back to Kat. Her breathing was shallow, and her skin was clammy to the touch. He pressed his hand against the wound on her arm, trying to stem the bleeding.

"Stay with me, Kat," he shouted, trying to be heard over the sound of gunfire and the truck's engine. "We're almost out of here."

Her eyes opened again, struggling to focus on Mike's face. "You...always made dates exciting," she whispered.

Mike swallowed hard, fighting back the surge of emotions threatening to overwhelm him. "Always," he said fiercely. "Would you call this a date though?"

A ghost of a smile tugged at her lips before her eyes closed again.

The truck bounced violently as Cooper navigated the rough terrain, trying to put as much distance between them and their pursuers as possible. He braced himself against the door, doing his best to keep her stable.

"How is she?" called Cooper over his shoulder, glancing between the road ahead and the rearview mirror.

"Not good," said Mike grimly. "We need to get her to a hospital."

Cooper nodded. "There's a clinic about twenty miles north. It's our best bet."

He glanced out the rear window. Two SUVs were in hot pursuit, gaining ground. "We've got company."

"I see them." Cooper tightened his grip on the steering wheel.

In the bed of the truck, Viper and Sawyer continued to exchange fire with their pursuers. The sharp crack of gunshots punctuated the air, accompanied by the ping of bullets ricocheting off metal.

"We're sitting ducks out here." Sawyer shouted.

Mike searched for a solution. They couldn't outrun the cartel vehicles forever, and Kat's condition was deteriorating by the minute. If anything happened to Viper or Sawyer, Sage and Kinsey would be devastated and angry that they'd driven off without even a brief explanation or quick goodbye.

"Cooper, take the next turn." He had an idea forming. "Head for the ravine."

Cooper's eyes widened in understanding. "You sure about this?"

He nodded grimly. "It's our only shot."

As they approached the turn, he braced himself, holding her securely. Cooper yanked the wheel hard, sending the truck careening down a narrow dirt path that led toward a deep ravine.

The pursuing vehicles followed, their drivers perhaps too focused on the chase to realize where they were headed. As they neared the edge of the ravine, Cooper slammed on the brakes, bringing the truck to a screeching halt mere feet from the precipice.

"Now," shouted Mike.

Cooper threw the truck into reverse, gunning the engine. The tires spun, kicking up a cloud of dust and gravel. For a heart-stopping moment, Mike feared they wouldn't have enough traction.

Then the truck lurched backward, just as the first cartel vehicle crested the rise. Unable to stop in time, it plunged over the edge of the ravine, disappearing from view. The second vehicle managed to swerve, but in doing so, it flipped onto its side, sliding to a stop in a shower of sparks.

"Move," said Mike urgently.

Cooper didn't need to be told twice. He threw the truck back into drive and sped away, leaving the wreckage behind them. As the adrenaline of the chase began to fade, he turned his attention back to Kat. Her pulse was weak, and her skin was alarmingly pale. He pressed his hand more firmly against her wound, willing the bleeding to stop while wondering if she was bleeding internally too. He lifted her shirt and saw the ugly bruises on her ribs. They could have punctured her lung.

"Hang on, Kat," he whispered, his voice thick with emotion. "We're almost there."

The miles seemed to crawl by as they raced toward the clinic. His injured arm throbbed, but he barely noticed, all his focus on the woman lying unconscious across him. Finally, the small medical facility came into view. Cooper screeched to a halt in front of the entrance, and Mike was out of the truck before it had fully stopped, cradling Kat in his arms.

"Help," he shouted as he burst through the doors. "We need a doctor."

Medical staff rushed forward, quickly assessing the situation. They gently took Kat from Mike's arms, placing her on a gurney and whisking her away.

As the doors swung shut behind them, he stood rooted to the spot, his heart hammering in his chest. The fear and uncertainty of the past hours crashed over him like a wave, leaving him feeling hollow and drained.

A hand on his shoulder startled him from his thoughts. He turned to find Cooper standing beside him, concern etched on his weathered face.

"She's tough, Mike," said Cooper quietly. "She'll pull through."

Mike nodded, unable to find his voice. As the adrenaline faded, the pain in his arm flared to life, reminding him of his own injury.

Cooper noticed his grimace. "Come on, brother. Let's get you patched up while we wait for news on Kat."

As a nurse led him to an examination room, Mike's thoughts remained with Kat. He had come so close to losing her today. The realization hit him hard, bringing with it a clarity he hadn't felt in years. He loved her. He had never stopped loving her, and if given the chance, he would spend the rest of his life making up for the mistakes of the past.

But first, Kat had to survive. He closed his eyes, sending up a silent prayer to whatever higher power might be listening. *Please*, he thought desperately. *Please let her be okay.*

As the nurse began cleaning his wound, he braced himself for the long wait ahead. Whatever happened, he would be there for Kat. He had failed her once before, but he wouldn't make that mistake again.

The hours crawled by as Mike and his team waited for news on Kat's condition. The small waiting room of the clinic felt suffocating, the air thick with tension and unspoken fears. He paced restlessly, his newly bandaged arm throbbing in time with his racing heartbeat.

Cooper sat in a corner, his prosthetic leg stretched out before him, eyes closed but posture alert. Viper and Sawyer stood guard near the entrance, their vigilant gazes sweeping the area for any sign of threat.

Finally, a doctor emerged from the treatment area, his expression grave. Mike's heart leapt into his throat as he rushed forward.

"How is she?" he demanded, his voice hoarse with worry.

The doctor hesitated, his brow furrowing. "She's stable, but her condition is serious. It looks like she had a bad fall, and there was internal bleeding, causing significant blood loss. We've managed to repair the damage somehow." He frowned. "You should have taken her to a major trauma center, not a rural hospital."

"You were closest," said Cooper without looking up.

"Yes, I suppose we are."

"How is she?" asked Mike impatiently. "Is she going to be okay?"

The doctor hesitated for a second that felt like eternity. "I'll cautiously say yes, but the next twenty-four hours will be critical."

His knees felt weak with relief and renewed fear. "Can I see her?"

The doctor nodded. "Briefly. She needs rest."

As Mike followed the doctor down the sterile hallway, his mind raced with all the things he wanted to say to Kat. Apologies, declarations of love, promises for the future—they all clamored for attention, threatening to overwhelm him. When he stepped into her room and saw her lying there, gray and fragile against the stark white sheets that emphasized the darkness of her hair and how washed-out she was, all words fled. He moved to her bedside, gently taking her hand in his.

"I'm here, Kat," he whispered, his voice thick with emotion. "I'm not going anywhere."

Chapter 3—Mike

TWO DAYS LATER, MIKE maneuvered through the doorway of Cooper's ranch house, cradling Kat's battered form in his arms. Her head lolled against his chest, dark curls spilling over his forearm. The familiar scent of her coconut shampoo mingled with antiseptic reached his now, an unwelcome reminder of the ordeal she'd endured.

"Easy now," he murmured, navigating the narrow hallway to the guest room. Sunlight streamed through the windows, illuminating dust motes dancing in the air. The floorboards creaked beneath his feet, each step deliberate and careful.

Kat's eyes fluttered open as he lowered her onto the bed. "Mike?" Her voice was raspy, barely above a whisper.

"I'm here," he said, arranging the pillows behind her head. "You're safe now."

She winced as she shifted, her hand instinctively moving to her bandaged side. "Where are we?"

"Cooper's ranch," he said, pulling up a chair beside the bed. "It's the safest place for you right now. When the doc at the tiny hospital learned you'd possibly been injured by the cartel, he told us to get you outta there." He stroked his beard. "I'm not sure if he was protecting your or the hospital, but he assured us you're stable and gave us meds. You have to rest for a bit though, and you've never been good at that."

She glanced around the room, taking in the weathered dresser and faded curtains. Kat's eyes darted around the room, lingering on the weathered dresser and the faded curtains. Mike watched as her lips curled into a weak smile, her gaze seeming to search for something to say. She looked worn out, fragile.

"It's...cozy," she finally muttered.

Mike shifted forward, elbows bracing against his knees. His throat felt tight, his mind a whirlwind of everything unsaid between them. "Kat, I..." His words stalled, frustration at his own inability to articulate what he needed to say building in his chest. "I'm glad you're okay. When I got that call, I thought—"

"I know," she cut him off, her voice low, almost apologetic. "Thank you for coming for me."

The silence between them stretched, awkward and heavy, like all the years of regrets sitting in the space between their bodies. Mike cleared his throat, trying to break the tension.

"Do you need anything? Water? More painkillers?" His voice came out rougher than intended.

Kat shook her head, her face still somewhat grayish under the dim lighting. "No, I'm fine. Just...tired." She hesitated for a beat, her brow contracting as if deciding something. "I need to tell you about what happened."

Mike nodded.

"How'd you know it was probably the cartel after me?" she asked, looking at him with a tired sort of curiosity.

"Sawyer spotted some matching neck tattoos during the first shootout. It was a guess, but a good one considering where it all went down."

She nodded like that piece of information connected dots in her mind. "I don't know if they're cartel, affiliated with them, or just another group of criminals."

His hands clenched as he leaned closer.

She took a deep breath, wincing at the motion, and he resisted the urge to tell her to take it easy. "I was flying my usual route," she said, her voice shaky, "When I saw something strange. A bunch of vehicles—way out in the middle of nowhere, near the border."

Mike's jaw tightened. He could see the scene in his mind—the desert stretch and the isolation. Something bad always followed.

"There were people...so many people." Her voice cracked, and he didn't miss the tremble in her words. "Even kids. Then...gunshots."

His stomach dropped as he involuntarily tightened his fists. "A massacre?"

She nodded, her deep brown eyes shining with unshed tears. His heart twisted. He hated seeing her like this. "I couldn't just fly away. I had to do something. I kept hearing my father's voice."

Mike's chest tightened with the mention of her father. He gave her a small, melancholy smile. The old man had been a moral compass for both of them, always talking about doing the right thing, no matter how hard it was. Mike had admired him, maybe even more so than his own dad. He'd passed before the IED had taken everything from Mike and led to the divorce, so he hadn't learned of Mike's ultimate failure. "Joel's piece about doing what's right, even when it isn't easy?"

She nodded again, her voice quiet. "Yeah. So I landed. That's when I found her. Maria."

"Maria?" The name startled him. "Was someone with you? Who was she?"

Kat's face scrunched in pain, both physical and emotional. "She's dead now, but she was a survivor...for a while."

A figurative pit opened in his gut. She hadn't saved the woman. Damn it. He could see the strain in her eyes as she pushed through the memory. "She was hiding and terrified. I tried to help her escape, but..." Her voice faltered for a moment before she shut her eyes, like if she didn't see him, she could hold back the tears.

Without thinking, he reached out, his hand hesitating in the air for a second before he gently took hers. He felt the coldness of her fingers, fragile against his. He wanted to say something to make it better, but there were no words for this. He knew well how crushing it was to fail in a mission to save someone. He'd never expected his commercial-pilot wife to have to endure such a thing.

Ex-wife, reminded a bitter voice in the back of his head.

Kat squeezed his hand, pulling herself together. "We ran and hid in a cave for a couple of hours until dark, but they were everywhere. Maria got hit. She told me to leave her—to save myself." Her grip tightened around Mike's fingers, and his heart broke with her next words. "I didn't want to leave her, Mike. I swear I didn't want to, but she…died. She seemed almost relieved…like she wanted to be with her husband and son again. They were killed in the massacre." A sob finally broke free, visibly cracking the wall she'd built around herself.

Mike gave her shoulder a firm but gentle pat. "You did everything you could. You tried to help her, Kat. You did more than most people would've."

She let out a bitter laugh, her voice thick with frustration. "Tried and failed." Her eyes hardened as her jaw set. "We can't let more people die like that. We have to stop Los Coyotes."

Mike shook his head, heart sinking. She was still so fired up, so damn determined, and she was barely hanging on by a thread. "Kat, you're in no shape to—"

"I made her a promise," she interrupted, her voice defiant as she tried to sit up, only to wince and fall back into the pillows.

"Easy." He placed his hand on her uninjured shoulder, guiding her back down. "You need to rest. I'm not dismissing your promise, but right now, you need to focus on healing."

Her muscles relaxed, and he could see the exhaustion starting to overtake her.

She looked at him, her voice small, almost pleading. "You believe me, don't you? About what I saw?"

Mike's gaze softened. "Of course I do. We'll get to the bottom of this. I'll help you take down this Los Coyotes if I can." The doubt lingered in his mind though. Taking down a group like Los Coyotes, whom he inferred were human smugglers, wasn't some small-time operation. But he couldn't deny her when she looked at him like that.

She nodded, her eyelids drooping as her body finally gave in to the fatigue. "I'm sorry, Mike. For everything."

Mike swallowed, her words hitting him harder than he expected. "Me too, Kat. More than you know." He was talking about the lost years and suspected she was too.

Moments later, she drifted off to sleep, her breathing evening out. He remained by her side, lost in thought. The woman he had once loved—still loved, if he was honest with himself—had witnessed something horrific. Something that had nearly cost her her life, and now, as he watched her chest rise and fall with each breath, he made a silent vow to protect her, no matter the cost.

The sound of footsteps in the hallway jolted Mike from his reverie. Cooper appeared in the doorway. "How is she?"

He stood, scratching his beard absently. "Resting. She told me what happened, Coop. It's bad."

He nodded grimly. "I figured as much. Come on. The others are waiting. We need to talk."

With one last glance at Kat's sleeping form, Mike followed Cooper out of the room. Whatever storm was brewing on the horizon, they would face it as brothers. As a family.

Moments later, he paced the weathered floorboards of Cooper's living room, his mind racing with the information Kat had shared. The others gathered around with concern, sans their wives, but Mike was sure they'd all find ways to help too. Cooper leaned against the fireplace mantel, his prosthetic leg barely visible beneath his worn jeans.

"All right, Mike," said Cooper, his voice gruff. "What did Kat tell you?"

"She witnessed a massacre near the border. A group of vehicles, gunshots, and bodies everywhere. She tried to help a survivor named Maria escape, but they were pursued."

He leaned forward, his elbows resting on his knees. "Any idea who was behind it?"

"Not yet," said Mike, "But said Kat they were well-organized and heavily armed. This wasn't some random act of violence. She called them Los Coyotes."

Cooper nodded, his jaw clenched. "We need more information. I'm calling Clayton." As Cooper dialed, the room fell silent.

Mike's gaze drifted to the hallway leading to Kat's room, his chest tightening with worry and long-buried feelings. She'd be okay. She had to be.

Cooper's voice cut through the tension. "Clayton, it's Cooper. We need your help." He told him what had happened to Kat, and what she'd relayed, including the dead bodies and Maria's being in a separate location. "Can you use the satellite to scan an area near the Texas-Mexico border?" He paused, listening. "Yeah, that's right, and I need you to look into a group called Los Coyotes. See if you can find any connections."

The minutes ticked by as they waited for Clayton's response. Mike's fingers tapped an impatient rhythm on his thigh, conjuring worst-case scenarios.

Finally, Cooper's phone rang. He put it on speaker, and Clayton's voice filled the room. "I've got some information for you, but it's not good."

Mike's stomach dropped. "What did you find?"

"I located bloodstains on the ground in a couple of locations," said Clayton, his tone grim.

Sawyer frowned. "You had boots on the ground?"

Clayton gave a short laugh. "No. The satellite tech can damned near give you a colonoscopy from space these days, Sawyer."

"Great," said Viper without enthusiasm.

"I'm assuming the huge puddle were the first victims. The smaller stains are in line with blood loss from one victim. It's hard to say in total, but I'd say at least ten people died there."

A heavy silence fell over the room before Clayton continued, "There's more. Los Coyotes? They're affiliated with the Gutiérrez cartel. They give the cartel a cut of their profits for use of the cartel corridors."

Sawyer cursed under his breath. "The same cartel R-7 and Mitch were mixed up with?"

"The very same," Clayton confirmed. "These guys are bad news, and now that Maria's dead, Kat is the only witness left."

They traded uneasy looks, the risks unspoken but understood by all. His fists clenched at his sides as a fierce protectiveness surged through him.

Cooper's voice was hard "Thanks, Clayton. We'll take it from here."

As the call ended, the men exchanged grim looks. Viper, who had been silent throughout, spoke up. "We need to fortify the ranch. They'll come for her, and we need to be ready."

"They might not find her here," said Mike with more hope than conviction.

"They'll come," said Sawyer. "They probably have their own satellites, or access to someone who can give them information. It's only a matter of time before they track us here."

Cooper nodded. "Agreed. Mike, you stay with Kat. The rest of us will start preparing."

As the others filed out, he lingered in the living room, his mind whirling. He'd pushed Kat away once before, thinking he was protecting her from his own demons. Now, faced with a very real threat to her life, he vowed not to make the same mistake again.

He made his way back to Kat's room, pausing in the doorway. She stirred, her eyes fluttering open. "Mike? What's going on?"

He crossed the room, settling into the chair beside her bed. "We've got some news, Kat, but first, how are you feeling?"

She pushed herself up, wincing slightly. "Better, I think. Still sore, but the pain's not as bad." She searched his face. "What aren't you telling me, Mike?"

He took a deep breath, steeling himself. "Clayton confirmed enough blood for several victims, though the bodies were long gone."

She squeezed his hand. After a moment, she composed herself, her expression hardening. "What else did Clayton find out?"

Mike hesitated, not wanting to burden her with more bad news, but she deserved the truth. "The group responsible for the massacre? They're affiliated with the Gutiérrez cartel."

Kat's eyes widened. "So, they are cartel? What have I gotten myself into?"

He leaned closer, his voice low and firm. "Listen to me, Kat. We're going to keep you safe. The whole brotherhood is here, and we're fortifying the ranch. They won't get to you."

She nodded, but he could see the fear lingering in her eyes. "What do we do now?"

"Now," said Mike, standing up, "We prepare. Can you walk?"

Kat swung her legs over the side of the bed, testing her strength. "I think so. Just...give me a hand?"

He helped her to her feet, supporting her as she took a few tentative steps. Her body was warm against his, and he fought to keep his focus on the task at hand. It had been far too long since he'd held her like this, with her soft curves against him, and his cock responded predictably, but he tried to ignore it.

As they made their way out of the room, the sound of hammering and power tools filled the air. Cooper's voice rang out, issuing orders to the others.

"Looks like they've already started," she said, taking in the flurry of activity.

Mike nodded. "Cooper doesn't waste time. Come on. Let's see where we can help."

They stepped onto the porch, the Texas sun beating down on them. Sawyer and Viper were reinforcing the windows, while Cooper oversaw the installation of additional security cameras. Kinsey and Nina had joined the crew to help pass material. They waved to Kat and him but couldn't drop what they were holding.

Cooper caught sight of them and made his way over. "Kat, good to see you on your feet. How are you holding up?"

She managed a small smile. "I'm okay, Cooper. Thanks for everything you're doing."

He waved off her thanks. "You're family, Kat. We take care of our own."

As he filled them in on the security measures being implemented, Mike's mind drifted to the battles that lay ahead. The cartel wouldn't give up easily, and Kat's safety hung in the balance.

He glanced at her, taking in her determined expression despite the pallor of her skin with its still faintly ashy undertone. She was strong and always had been. It was one of the things he loved about her.

Love. The word echoed in his mind, bringing with it a rush of emotions he'd long tried to suppress. Now, faced with the possibility of losing her, he couldn't run from his feelings any longer. He would protect Kat, not just from the cartel, but from the pain he'd caused her in the past, and when this was all over, if they both made it through, he'd find a way to make things right between them.

Chapter 4—Kat

KAT STIRRED IN THE guest room bed, her body aching with every movement. The soft sunlight filtering through the curtains illuminated Mike's silhouette as he sat vigilant by her side. His presence both comforted and confused her.

"You're still here," she mumbled, her voice hoarse from disuse.

Mike leaned forward, his eyes filled with concern. "Of course, I am. I'm not leaving you."

She attempted to sit up, wincing as pain shot through her ribs. Mike quickly moved to assist her, his strong hands gentle as he adjusted the pillows behind her back.

"Easy there," he cautioned. "The doctor said you need to take it slowly, and you were up too much earlier as it was."

She nodded, settling back against the pillows. "How long have I been out?"

"A few hours. You about collapsed into bed." He smiled. "It reminded me of that time you got so drunk on New Year's Eve, just before our second anniversary..."

She groaned, remembering that night of fun, and the raging headache the next day. Pushing aside her embarrassment that still lingered years later, she studied his face, noting the dark circles under his eyes, and the disheveled state of his brunette beard and hair. "Have you slept at all?"

He shrugged, a wry smile tugging at his lips. "Caught a few winks here and there. Nothing to worry about."

She frowned. "You need rest too."

"I'm fine," he said stubbornly. "What matters is that you're safe and recovering."

She sighed, frustration bubbling up inside her. "Why did you bring me here, Mike? We've been divorced for years. You don't owe me anything."

His expression softened as a flicker of pain crossing his features. "Kat, I—"

"No," she interrupted, her voice growing stronger. "I want the truth. Why did you leave me after your injuries? Why push me away only to come rushing back now?"

He tensed, clenching his hands into fists on his lap. He stood abruptly, pacing the small room like a caged animal. "You don't understand."

"Then make me understand," she said, following his movements with her gaze. "I deserve that much, don't I?"

He stopped at the window, his back to her as he stared out at the Texas landscape. The silence stretched between them, heavy with unspoken words and painful memories. Finally, he turned to face her, expression revealing guilt and anguish. "I thought I was protecting you."

Her heart clenched at the raw emotion in his words. "Protecting me from what?"

He took a deep breath, steeling himself for the confession. "From me. From the monster I'd become after Afghanistan." He moved closer to the bed, sinking into the chair beside her. "Do you remember that night, about a month after I came home?"

She slowly nodded, a flicker of recognition in her eyes. "You had a nightmare. I tried to wake you, and—"

"And I lashed out," he finished, his voice thick with self-loathing. "I struck your shoulder, Kat. My own wife."

She reached for his hand. "It was an accident. You were trapped in a nightmare. I never blamed you for that."

He shook his head vehemently. "But I blamed myself. I saw the bruise on your skin the next morning, and I couldn't risk hurting you again. The PTSD, the nightmares, and the constant pain—it was all too much. I thought you'd be better off without me."

Tears welled up in Kat's eyes as the truth of his words sank in. She'd suspected that was the reason he'd changed so much, but hearing confirmation was like a weight lifting off her heart. "So you pushed me away," she whispered.

Mike nodded, his grip on her hand tightening. "I thought I was doing the right thing. I convinced myself that you deserved better than a broken man, who couldn't even guarantee your safety in your own bed."

She cupped his cheek with her free hand, forcing him to meet her gaze. "You idiot," she said softly, a sad smile playing on her lips. "Did it ever occur to you that I might have wanted to help you through it? That I loved you enough to face those trials together?"

He leaned into her touch, closing his eyes briefly. "I was too proud and too scared. I couldn't bear the thought of hurting you again, physically or emotionally. So I did what I thought was best—I let you go."

She shook her head, tears now flowing freely down her cheeks. "And look where that got us. Years of pain and loneliness, all because you couldn't trust me with your struggles."

He opened his eyes, his gaze intense as he looked at her. "I made a mistake, Kat. When I heard you were in danger, I couldn't ignore how much I still care about you. I can't bear the thought of losing you for good."

His breath hitched at his admission. "What happens now, Mike?"

He brought her hand to his lips, pressing a gentle kiss to her knuckles. "Now, I'm here for as long as you'll have me. I want to make things right, if you'll let me."

She searched his face, seeing the sincerity in his eyes. "It won't be easy. We've both changed, and there's a lot of hurt to work through."

He nodded solemnly. "I know, but I'm willing to try if you are. No more running away, and no more pushing you out. I want to face whatever comes next together."

Warmth spread through her chest from a glimmer of hope she hadn't allowed herself to feel in years. "Okay," she whispered. "We'll take it one day at a time."

He flashed a tentative smile and nodded. "Starting with getting you back on your feet."

Kat nodded, suddenly feeling depleted from the emotional conversation. "Will you stay?" she asked, her eyelids growing heavy.

Mike squeezed her hand gently. "I'm not going anywhere, Kat. I promise."

As she drifted off to sleep, she was more peaceful than she'd felt in years despite the cartel threat looming over her. They had a long road ahead, but they might actually have a chance at rebuilding what they had lost.

KAT WOKE JUST AS DAWN broke, the light faint through the curtains. Mike sat beside her, his body crammed awkwardly into the small chair, looking uncomfortable but steadfast. She shook her head. "You could've shared the bed."

He blinked, startled by her voice. His brow wrinkled as he stretched, his stiff posture clearly making him ache. "I'm not risking reinjuring you."

She sighed but didn't argue, knowing how obstinate he could be. His protectiveness hadn't dulled over the years. Now that her mind was clearer, she shifted to what really mattered. "Did you finish preparing the ranch?"

Mike rubbed a hand over his face, the scruff on his chin rasping under his fingers. "Cooper and the others are working on it. Fences, cameras, and lookout points. We're covering all the bases."

Kat nodded, trying to piece together the half-remembered details from yesterday. The fog of painkillers still lingered in her system. "So...we're safe here?"

He pushed himself to his feet, walking to the window to stare at the Texas landscape, his broad shoulders tense. "We're doing everything we can. Cooper's reinforced the perimeter, and we've set up extra security measures. No one's getting in without us knowing."

Kat watched the way his muscles tightened as he spoke. "What about weapons? Do we have enough if they show up?"

Mike turned, his expression grim. "We've got plenty. Cooper's been stockpiling for years, and Viper and Sawyer brought more when they arrived. We're ready for whatever comes."

He moved back toward the chair, sitting heavily like the weight of their situation pressed down on him. "We've also got radios and code words in case things go sideways."

She leaned her head back against the pillow, relieved by how thorough they'd been. "What about an escape plan? If things get bad, we need a way out."

A small smile tugged at the corner of his mouth. "You always think three steps ahead. Cooper's got escape routes mapped out. Vehicles hidden in strategic spots, full tanks, and ready to go."

He leaned in slightly, lowering his voice like someone might overhear. "We've also reached out to some of our old military contacts. If we need backup, we can call in favors."

Kat's eyes widened. "You're really not messing around."

Mike shook his head, his face serious. "We can't. These guys don't play by any rules. They've got resources and manpower, and they'll do whatever it takes. Depending on how deep their ties with Los Coyotes run, we might be facing more than just traffickers."

His hand hovered in the air for a second before it landed on hers. He squeezed gently. "I promise we'll do whatever it takes to keep you safe. I won't let them get to you."

Her throat tightened as she squeezed his hand back, ignoring the twinge of pain the movement caused. "I trust you."

The silence between them grew thick, full of unspoken feelings, memories from another life. Mike cleared his throat and broke the moment. "There's more. We've been talking to some of our old military contacts. They're feeding us intel on cartel movements."

Her eyebrows shot up in surprise. "You still have those connections?"

Mike gave a small, humorless laugh. "Some ties don't break, especially when lives are on the line. That network's kept us ahead of a lot of dangers before."

He stood up, pacing the room. His limp was more noticeable now, likely from fatigue, but it didn't slow him down. "According to our sources, the cartel's planning something big in this area. Expanding their smuggling routes. They won't want witnesses, and if Los Coyotes mentions you..."

Kat's heart raced, the reality of her situation sinking in. "They won't stop until they find me."

Mike stopped mid-pace, his expression fierce as he turned to her. "They'll try, but they're going to have to get through all of us first. We're not just sitting back waiting for them. If they come, they'll regret it. If I have to, I'll take the fight to them and burn it all down."

Kat studied him for a moment, seeing the man she had once loved with all her heart—the protector and warrior who'd do anything to make things right. "I want to help," she said firmly, her voice steady.

Mike shook his head. "You need to heal. You've been through hell, and I'm not letting you jump back into the fire."

She winced as she shifted, the dull ache in her ribs reminding her of how fragile she was. but her mind was clear. "I'm not sitting this out,

Mike. I'm injured, but I can help. Strategy, communications—whatever you need."

He opened his mouth, clearly ready to argue, but she cut him off before he could speak. "Don't try to sideline me, Michael Deacon. We're in this together. Just like old times."

A slow smile spread across his face, his eyes shining with something close to admiration. "I should've known better than to try and keep you out of it. You've always been the most stubborn woman I've ever met."

She grinned, though it pulled painfully at her cheek. "Don't forget it. Tell me more about what you've gathered. I want to know everything."

His smile faded into a more serious expression as he nodded. "All right, but let's get you something to eat first. You'll need your strength."

He stood to leave, his hand resting on the doorknob, but Kat's voice stopped him.

"Mike?"

He turned, his face softening. "Yeah?"

"Thank you for being here."

He met her gaze, something unspoken lingering between them. "Always."

With that, he stepped out of the room, leaving her alone to process everything. The Los Coyotes and possible cartel involvement threat still hung over her, but she was more hopeful than she'd been. Maybe they had a shot—not just at survival, but at reclaiming what they had lost.

Chapter 5—Kat

ALMOST A WEEK LATER, she stepped into the bustling kitchen, the aroma of cooking bacon and freshly brewed coffee filling her senses. Nina stood at the stove, expertly flipping pancakes while Kinsey scrambled eggs in a large skillet. Sage was slicing fruit at the counter, her purple curls bouncing as she moved.

"Need an extra pair of hands?" asked Kat, rolling up her sleeves.

Nina turned, a warm smile lighting up her face. "Absolutely. Could you start on the toast? There's a loaf of sourdough in the breadbox."

As Kat moved to the counter, a sense of belonging washed over her. It had been years since she'd been part of a family, not since her divorce from Mike. Her father had been her only other family after her mother's death when she was young. The easy camaraderie between these women was something she'd missed without realizing it.

Kinsey glanced over her shoulder, her eyes twinkling. "So, Kat, how are you holding up after everything that's happened?"

Kat paused, considering her answer as she sliced the bread. "Honestly? I'm still processing it all, but being here, with all of you, helps."

Sage nodded, understanding in her eyes. "We've all been through our own hells, but we're stronger together."

As they worked, the women fell into an easy rhythm, chatting and laughing. Kat found herself opening up, sharing stories of her life as a pilot and the adventures she'd had.

"Wait," interrupted Nina, her eyes wide. "You flew through a tropical storm once? Just to deliver supplies?"

Kat grinned, remembering the exhilaration of that flight. "It was touch and go for a while. The turbulence was so bad I thought my teeth would rattle out of my head, but those people needed the medical supplies, and I wasn't about to let a little bad weather stop me."

Kinsey whistled, impressed. "Damn, girl. You've got some serious guts."

As they finished preparing the meal, Kat felt a warmth in her chest that had nothing to do with the hot stove. These women, who had welcomed her into their circle without hesitation, were becoming more than just allies. They were becoming friends, and she let herself imagine them becoming more like family if she and Mike reconciled as she hoped.

The men joined them as they set the table, the kitchen filled with the sounds of chairs scraping and plates clinking. Mike caught Kat's eye as he entered, giving her a small smile. It caused a flutter in her stomach from memories of their past mingling with the uncertain present.

As the discussion continued, she studied the faces around the table. These people, brought together by circumstances beyond their control, had formed a bond that went beyond friendship. They were a family, forged in adversity and strengthened by shared experiences. It left her envious.

Nina reached out, squeezing Kat's hand. "You okay?" she asked softly.

Kat nodded, surprised to find tears pricking at the corners of her eyes. "Yeah, I just... I haven't had this in a long time. A family, I mean."

Nina's smile was gentle. "Well, you've got one now. Whether you like it or not."

The table erupted in laughter, the tension of their earlier discussion momentarily forgotten. She wiped tears from her eyes, her sides aching from laughing so hard.

As the laughter died down, Mike caught Kat's her gaze from across the table. For a moment, she allowed herself to remember the good times they'd shared, before his injuries and PTSD had driven them apart.

Cooper's voice brought her back to the present. "Let's talk logistics. We need to do the daily perimeter check. Viper, I want you to do that today. Trade off with Sawyer, in case he's missed something."

Viper nodded. "On it. I'll take Sawyer with me, and we can compare notes."

Sawyer nodded his agreement, his mouth too full of pancakes to speak.

"Nina, Kinsey," Cooper continued, "I need you to inventory our supplies. Food, medical, ammunition—everything. We need to know exactly what we're working with."

The women nodded.

Cooper turned to Kat, his eyes assessing. "Kat, I know you're a pilot, but how are you with communications?"

Kat straightened, feeling a sense of purpose. "I'm pretty good. I've had to handle all kinds of radio systems in my work."

He nodded, appearing satisfied. "Good. I want you to set up a communications hub, probably in the barn. It's already a control room of sorts. We need to be able to monitor police bands, emergency frequencies...everything. If the coyote whelps or the cartel make a move, I want to know about it before they do."

As everyone began to disperse, carrying their plates to the sink, a hand touched her arm. She turned to find Mike standing close, his eyes searching her face.

"Hey," he said softly. "Can we talk for a minute?"

She nodded, her heart racing. They stepped out onto the porch, the Texas sun already beating down hot enough to make her instantly start sweating despite the early hour.

He ran a hand through his hair, a gesture so familiar it made Kat's chest ache. "I just wanted to say... I'm glad you're here in spite of the crappy circumstances. I know things between us have been..."

"Complicated?" A wry smile tugged at her lips.

He chuckled. "Yeah, complicated, but seeing you here, working with the team... it reminds me of why I fell in love with you in the first place."

She forgot to take a breath for a second. She hadn't expected this or prepared herself for the rush of emotion his words would bring. "Mike, I—"

He held up a hand, his expression earnest. "You don't have to say anything. I just wanted you to know that I'm here. Whatever happens with the traffickers or the cartel... Whatever comes next, I've got your back."

Kat nodded, unable to find the words to express the mix of emotions swirling inside her. Instead, she reached out, squeezing his hand.

The screen door creaked open behind them, and Sage poked out her head. "Hey, lovebirds," she called, a teasing lilt in her voice. "We've got work to do. You can make googly eyes at each other later."

Mike laughed. "All right. We're coming."

As they turned to head back inside, Kat caught sight of the others through the window. Nina and Kinsey were bent over a notebook, making lists as Sage settled the kids in the living room with toys. Viper and Sawyer were studying a map of the property, their heads close together as they discussed strategy. Cooper stood at the center of it all, his presence radiating strength and determination.

With a nod to Mike, she stepped back into the house. The cartel might be coming for them, but they would be ready. Together, they were stronger than any threat that could come their way.

Chapter 6—Mike

A FEW DAYS LATER, MIKE crouched behind a stack of hay bales, scanning the horizon. The setting sun made it harder to see, casting long shadows across Cooper's ranch. The beauty of the scene was marred by the unmistakable sound of approaching vehicles. They'd been expecting it thanks to chatter Kat had intercepted in the makeshift comms room in the barn.

"They're here," he said into his radio. "At least three trucks coming in from the south."

Cooper's voice crackled through the speaker. "Copy that. Everyone in position?"

Mike glanced around, spotting Viper and Sawyer at their designated posts. He gave a quick thumbs up, which they returned. "Affirmative. We're ready."

The rumble of engines grew louder as the cartel's vehicles approached. Mike's fingers tightened around his rifle, but he steadied his breathing. The first truck burst through the fence line, sending splinters of wood flying. Two more followed close behind, their occupants already leaning out of windows with guns at the ready.

"Now." Cooper's voice rang out.

Mike squeezed the trigger, his shots joining the stridency of gunfire that erupted from multiple directions. The lead truck's tires exploded, sending it careening into a ditch. The other two vehicles screeched to a halt, cartel members pouring out like angry hornets from a disturbed nest.

"Mike, on your six," shouted Viper.

Mike spun around, narrowly avoiding a bullet that whistled past his ear. He returned fire, dropping the attacker with two quick shots to the chest. The acrid smell of gunpowder filled the air, mixing with the earthy scent of the ranch.

"Sawyer, watch your flank," he called out, spotting movement to his friend's left.

Sawyer pivoted, taking down the approaching invader with practiced efficiency, but as he turned back, another attacker emerged from behind a tractor. The sound of a gunshot rang out, and Sawyer stumbled backward, clutching his shoulder.

"Man down," Mike shouted into his radio. "Sawyer's hit." Without hesitation, he broke cover, sprinting toward his fallen comrade. Bullets whizzed past him, kicking up dirt at his feet. He could hear Viper providing covering fire, the steady rhythm of his shots a reassuring backdrop.

He reached Sawyer, grabbing him by his good arm. "Come on, brother. We're getting you out of here."

Viper appeared at Sawyer's other side, and together, they half-dragged him toward the relative safety of the barn. Sawyer's face was pale, his teeth clenched against the pain.

"How bad?" asked Mike as they moved.

Sawyer grimaced. "Just a flesh wound. I'll live."

As they neared the barn, the radio crackled to life. Kinsey's voice came through, tight with worry. This time, their wives had refused to stay at Sawyer's, so they were in the safe room while Kat monitored communications from the barn "Is Sawyer okay? What happened?"

Mike keyed his radio. "He's hit, but it doesn't look too serious. We're getting him to safety now."

There was a pause before Kinsey's voice returned, steel in her tone. "Guys, you hearing this? Shoot the bastard who shot my husband."

"With pleasure," said Cooper.

From his position, Mike couldn't see Cooper, but he heard the sharp crack of his rifle. A moment later, one of the bogeys dropped. He saw it peripherally before turning his attention back to their task.

They pushed into the barn, where Kat was waiting, medical supplies ready, her face tense but composed. She quickly motioned toward the table she had set up.

"Get him on the table," she said, her voice calm despite everything happening outside.

Mike and Viper hefted Sawyer onto the table. He winced as he settled on his back, but he managed a pained grin. "Just a flesh wound. I'll live."

Kat didn't waste time. She tore open gauze and antiseptic with precision, pressing down on the wound as blood seeped through. Her hands moved quickly, being efficient despite the panic Mike could see flickering behind her eyes. She was holding it together.

As she worked, he turned to Viper, wiping sweat from his brow. "We need to get back out there. Cooper can't hold them off alone."

Viper nodded, his single eye gleaming with determination. "Let's go make sure these bastards know whose house they're in."

Mike grabbed his rifle, nodding at Kat as he moved toward the door. "Keep him stable. We'll be back."

Kat glanced up, her gaze locking with his for a split second. "Be careful."

Mike gave her a tight nod before turning back to Viper. The sounds of gunfire had intensified outside, and the air inside the barn felt suffocating with tension. He checked his weapon as they headed toward the entrance.

As soon as they burst out of the barn, Mike's world narrowed to the rhythm of battle—aim, fire, and reload. The sharp report of gunfire echoed in his ears, and his focus tunneled. Viper moved beside him, a blur of action as they fired on the encroachers trying to advance from the tree line. The night was alive with the sounds of combat—shouts in both Spanish and English, the pop of rifles, and the occasional explosion from the grenades being lobbed toward the house.

A bullet grazed the arm that hadn't been nicked the day they rescued Kat, but the sting barely registered through the adrenaline. He spun, rifle already aimed, and took out the shooter with a single well-placed shot. Blood pounded in his ears, but he didn't slow down.

"Mike," Cooper's voice came through the radio. "They're trying to flank us from the east. Can you get to the windmill and provide overwatch?"

"On it." He was already moving, sprinting across the open ground toward the windmill. The field between the barn and the windmill was a gauntlet of flying bullets, but he zigzagged, keeping low as he dodged the hail of gunfire. His muscles screamed in protest, but he pushed through, finally reaching the metal framework.

He scrambled up the windmill, the metal cold beneath his hands as he climbed higher, his legs burning with the effort. The view from the top gave him a clear vantage point over the battlefield. He could see Cooper holding the line near the house, Viper providing suppressing fire behind an overturned tractor, and a group of invaders trying to outflank them sneaking along the tree line.

Mike steadied his breath, aimed carefully, and squeezed the trigger. One, two, three shots—each finding its mark. The group dropped before they even knew what hit them.

"East is clear," he said into the radio.

"Good work," Cooper's voice crackled back. "We've got more incoming from the north. Looks like they called for reinforcements."

Mike scanned the horizon, his heart sinking as he spotted another wave of vehicles approaching in the distance. Dust kicked up behind them, and the headlights of the trucks flickered in the darkness, growing larger as they barreled toward the ranch.

"How many?" he asked, tightening his grip on the rifle.

"Too damn many."

Mike watched the approaching vehicles, his mind racing. Reinforcements. This was going to get ugly fast. Just then, the radio crackled again, and Kat's voice came through, calm but determined.

"This is Kat. I've got eyes on those reinforcements. Want me to coordinate from here?"

Mike glanced toward the barn, knowing she was in there, keeping her cool. He admired the way she'd handled everything so far, but the thought of her in any more danger made his gut twist. Still, they needed her.

"Yeah," he said, breathing raggedly. "Keep us updated."

Her voice came back immediately. "Copy that. They're spreading out, but I'll guide you."

As she relayed the positions of the incoming traffickers, Mike focused on his role—taking out anyone who got close. He could see the trucks approaching, but there were more bodies on foot now, creeping in from all sides. They were outnumbered, but they weren't going down without a fight.

Suddenly, a shot rang out from below. Mike whipped his head around and saw one of the traffickers sneaking up behind Viper, gun raised. Without thinking, Mike lined up his shot and fired. The man dropped to the ground, his weapon clattering beside him.

Viper glanced up toward Mike's position and gave a quick nod. "Thanks for the save," his voice crackled through the radio.

"Stay sharp," he said, already scanning for the next target.

The minutes dragged on, every second feeling like an eternity. The firefight continued, a brutal, bloody clash between the cartel and the small but fierce group defending the ranch. Mike's arm throbbed where the bullet had grazed him earlier, but he couldn't afford to stop. Not yet.

"Mike," Kat's voice came through the radio again, this time more urgent. "More trucks coming in from the west. Looks like they're trying to circle around."

Mike's pulse quickened. He adjusted his position, scanning the tree line to the west, where the headlights of the new vehicles cut through the darkness. More reinforcements. They were relentless.

"Cooper, Viper, we've got more incoming from the west," Mike said into the radio. "They're trying to flank again."

Cooper's voice came back through, steady but grim. "We need to dig in. Let's make sure they don't get close enough to the barn or the house."

Mike nodded, his breath steadying as he focused on the horizon. They weren't going to let these bastards win. Not tonight.

"Kat," he said into the radio, "Keep us updated on their movements. We're going to need all the eyes we can get."

"Roger that."

"Thanks for the save." Viper's voice came through the radio.

"Anytime, brother." As the battle raged on, Mike had a surge of pride. Despite the odds, they were holding their ground. This ragtag family of former soldiers and the women who loved them was proving to be more than a match for the coyotes or the cartel. He still didn't know exactly who they were fighting.

Even as that thought crossed his mind, Mike saw something that made his blood run cold. A cartel member was making a beeline for the house—where Nina, Sage, Kinsey, and the children were hidden in the safe room Cooper had decided to add to the property sometime between Sawyer bringing Kinsey there and Viper arriving with Sage.

"Cooper," Mike shouted into his radio. "We've got a hostile heading for the house."

A burst of gunfire drowned out Cooper's reply. He watched in horror as the cartel member reached the porch, kicking in the front door. Without thinking, he swung down from the windmill, ignoring the burning in his muscles as he hit the ground running. He sprinted toward the house, dodging bullets and leaping over fallen bodies.

He burst through the front door, scanning the interior. The sound of pounding came from down the hall—the invader trying to break into the safe room.

Mike moved silently, years of training kicking in. He rounded the corner, raising his rifle.

The man turned, surprise flashing across his face, but before he could bring his own weapon to bear, Mike fired. The hostile dropped, his body slumping against the safe room door.

"It's clear," Mike called out.

The safe room door cracked open, Kinsey's worried face appearing. "Mike? Is it over?"

He shook his head. "Not yet, but we're winning. Stay put for now, okay? I've got to get back out there."

Kinsey nodded, looking scared but resolved. "Take care of everyone. Especially Sawyer."

Mike gave her a quick nod before turning back toward the front door. As he stepped onto the porch, he keyed his radio. "House is secure. Hostile is neutralized."

"Good work," said Cooper. "Now get your ass back out here. We're not done yet."

Mike's lips curved into a grim smile as he surveyed the battlefield. No, they weren't done, but they'd come out on top. They had to. There was too much at stake to fail now.

Chapter 7—Kat

KAT STOOD IN THE BARN gripping the radio headset, her heart racing as the sound of gunfire echoed through the walls. Sweat beaded on her brow, and the once-peaceful Texas landscape outside was now a battleground. The monitors in front of her flickered with the movement of cartel members advancing on Cooper's ranch. Billowing smoke obscured parts of the feed, and she had to steady her breathing with every explosion.

She pressed the radio button, striving to sound composed despite the chaos. "Mike, more vehicles are approaching from the east. Looks like at least three."

Through the crackling connection, Mike's voice came back, urgent. "We see them. Los Coyotes seems to have a never-ending stream of reinforcements." He left unspoken, but she inferred, that might be the strongest proof yet that the cartel was helping them.

Kat's stomach twisted as she stared at the monitors, watching the dust clouds rise behind the incoming trucks. The brotherhood had managed to hold off the initial attack, but these new arrivals were tipping the odds further against them. Tension built with every breath, knowing how close they were to being overrun.

Kat shifted her focus to the medical supplies she'd set up earlier. She'd just finished stabilizing Sawyer's wound, and he'd insisted on getting back out there, but she could already hear more gunfire outside. The men were stretched thin. She was stuck in the barn, coordinating as best she could, but every fiber of her being screamed to do more.

Her voice cut through the radio again. "Mike, Viper, you've got hostiles using the old barn for cover on the south side. Watch your flank."

The monitors showed the cartel members inching closer, darting between buildings as they tried to get closer to the main house. Kat clenched her fists, helpless to do anything but watch as Mike and Viper scrambled to reposition. The danger of the flanking maneuver was real, and it nearly left them exposed, but they managed to evade it just in time.

A sudden explosion on one of the monitors caught her attention—one of the cartel's vehicles went up in flames, metal flying in every direction. A small flicker of triumph sparked in her chest.

"Nice shot, Sawyer," said Viper through the radio, a rare note of satisfaction in his tone.

Kat allowed herself a moment to breathe, but the relief didn't last long. As the smoke cleared, more cartel members poured out from the remaining vehicles, their numbers overwhelming. She could see them moving in from all sides, their weapons trained on the house.

"This is bad," Kat muttered to herself, her gaze locked on the monitors as she watched the brotherhood fight off wave after wave of traffickers. They were holding their ground, but barely. She pressed the radio again, urgency creeping into her voice. "Guys, you're about to be overrun. We need to consider pulling back to a more defensible position."

Mike's reply came back, breathless but firm. "We're not giving up this ground, Kat. We just need to hold them off a little longer."

She gripped the edge of the desk as she watched the cartel forces close in. She wanted to argue, to tell him that falling back was the only option, but she knew Mike too well. He wasn't going to retreat with his family and the others depending on them to keep this place secure.

"Understood," she said, her voice sounding calmer than she felt. "I'll keep an eye on their movements. They're fanning out along the north side now."

Her gaze darted between the different camera feeds, trying to stay one step ahead. The invaders were relentless. The brotherhood was strong, but the sheer numbers made it clear this was a fight for survival.

Suddenly, the feed from one of the cameras flickered, and her heart sank as she saw a group of them slipping through a gap near the barn. They were trying to breach the back entrance.

"Mike, you've got movement near the back. They're trying to get into the barn," she warned, her voice woven with alarm.

She grabbed her sidearm, knowing she had to be ready. It had been a long time since she'd gone target shooting with her father, but she was sure it was like muscle memory. If they made it inside the barn, there wouldn't be much she could do, but she wasn't going to sit back and wait for them to find her. She moved toward the heavy door, bracing herself.

The radio crackled again. "We'll cover the back. Stay put, Kat," Mike's voice ordered.

Kat's heart raced as she watched the monitors, praying Mike and the others could hold the line. She could hear the gunfire intensifying outside, punctuated by the distant shouts of the cartel and the brotherhood's return fire. The sounds felt closer, more personal, as if the walls of the barn were closing in.

Every second felt like an eternity as she waited. The roar of engines and the crack of gunfire filled the air, blending into a chaotic symphony of violence that rattled her nerves. She wasn't a soldier. She had never fought on the front lines. Her instincts told her to run, to find somewhere safer, but there was nowhere else to go.

And she wasn't going to leave them.

Suddenly, the sound of rapid gunfire ripped through the air, and Kat's gaze shot back to the monitors. The cartel members who had tried to flank the barn were down. Mike and Cooper had intercepted them just in time. She let out a shaky breath.

"I've got them," Mike's voice came through the radio, steady but strained. "We're pushing them back."

She nodded to herself, forcing her heart to slow. She couldn't shake the worry gnawing at her, but she trusted Mike. She had to.

The sound of more vehicles approaching made her stomach drop. She could see the dust clouds rising in the distance as another wave of reinforcements closed in. There were too many of them—way too many.

"They're coming in from the west now," she said breathlessly. "You're going to be way too outnumbered soon."

"We'll handle it," said Mike, but even over the radio, she could hear the tension in his voice.

The minutes stretched on, the firefight outside growing more brutal with every passing moment. Her body was tense, her muscles aching from standing rigid for so long. She couldn't see a clear way out of this, but she couldn't let that fear take over. Not now. "You have to fall back," she said.

"Not yet," said Cooper, sounding impatient.

Kat opened her mouth to argue when a new voice cut through the radio chatter. "This is Clayton. I've got air support inbound. ETA three minutes. Hold your positions."

Relief flooded through Kat as she heard helicopters approaching from the north. "Help is on the way."

As the helicopters drew closer, Kat could see they were heavily armed. The lead chopper opened fire, its mini-gun tearing through the cartel's vehicles and sending the attackers scrambling for cover.

"That's what I call air support," said Sawyer with unrestrained joy over the radio.

Kat grinned, feeling a surge of hope as she watched the tide of battle turn. With Clayton's helicopters providing cover, the brotherhood was able to push back against the cartel forces.

"Kat, if you can see well enough, we need you to coordinate with the choppers," said Cooper. "Guide them to the most critical targets."

"Roger that," she said, her pilot's instincts kicking in as she began to direct the air support. It necessitated taking a pair of binoculars and a radio outside the relative safety of the barn, but she did it. "Chopper One, you've got a group of hostiles trying to flank from the east. Chopper Two, focus on the vehicles to the south. Cut off their escape route."

The next few minutes were a blur of action as Kat worked in tandem with Clayton's team. The invaders, caught between the brotherhood's ground fire and the relentless assault from above, began to falter.

"They're breaking," shouted Mike. "Push them back."

Kat watched with relief as the brotherhood surged forward, driving the remaining cartel forces away from the ranch house and surrounding area. The air was thick with dust and smoke, but through it all, she could see the tide had finally turned in their favor.

As the last of the cartel vehicles sped away, leaving their wounded and dead behind, a cheer went up from the ground. Her hands were shaking slightly as the adrenaline began to ebb.

"Nice work from up here, Kat," said Clayton, who was piloting one of the choppers himself. "My ground team is *en route* to secure the area and round up any stragglers. A buddy of mine in the DEA is officially taking point if they are cartel members. If not, another friend in ICE is ready to call in border patrol agents to make the arrest and has a Homeland Security investigator standing by."

"Thanks." She looked up in time to see Mike rushing toward her. She leapt forward to meet him, and they met halfway. He pulled her into a fierce embrace.

"You were amazing," he said, his voice muffled against her hair.

Kat allowed herself a moment to sink into his arms, the fear and tension of the past hours finally catching up with her. "We did it," she whispered. "We actually did it."

Mike pulled back, cupping her face in his hands. "We couldn't have done it without you, Kat."

She managed a tired smile. "You're being generous, but I'll let you."

Their moment was interrupted by the arrival of the others. Cooper limped toward them, his prosthetic leg clearly giving him trouble after the intense fight. Viper and Sawyer flanked him, all of them looking worse for wear but alive.

"Hell of a fight," said, clasping Kat's shoulder. "You did well."

Kat nodded, her throat tight with emotion. "Thanks, Coop. I'm just glad we all made it through."

Sawyer grinned despite the nasty gash on his forehead, and the blood soaking through the bandage on his arm. "Speak for yourself. I think I left a piece of my brain back there in the firefight."

Viper rolled his eyes. "Your brain was already missing a few pieces, Sawyer. This just evens you out."

Their banter was cut short by the arrival of Clayton's ground team. Heavily armed men in tactical gear swarmed the area, securing the perimeter and rounding up the surviving invaders.

Clayton himself approached the group after landing one of the choppers, his crisp uniform a stark contrast to their battle-worn appearance. "Good work, all of you. We've got the situation under control now. The aforementioned people will handle the cleanup and processing of the prisoners."

Cooper nodded. "Appreciate the assist, Clayton. We were in a tight spot there for a while."

Kat watched as Clayton moved among the captured Los Coyotes members, his keen gaze assessing each one. The tension in her shoulders eased slightly as she observed his confident demeanor. After several minutes, Clayton approached their group, his expression revealing satisfaction and relief.

"Good news," Clayton announced, his voice carrying across the dusty yard. "These guys are mostly low-level operatives. The cartel won't waste resources trying to recover them. They're loaners to Los Coyotes, so the cartel isn't actively involved beyond a surface level."

Mike stepped closer, his brow furrowed. "You sure about that, Clayton? They seemed pretty determined to take us out."

Clayton nodded, a wry smile playing at the corners of his mouth. "Trust me, I've seen this before. The Los Coyotes have become a liability now. They're going to be left to rot."

Kat's gaze drifted to the group of bound men sitting in the dirt. They scowled and looked tough, but she'd bet they were afraid. Good. "What happens to them now?" she asked, turning back to Clayton.

"I've called for an exfil team from ICE, since this is their jurisdiction, other than the straggler cartel members," he said, checking his watch. "They'll be here within the hour to take these guys into custody, and we'll let them sort out jurisdiction for which criminal. After that... Let's just say, they'll have plenty of time to reconsider their career choices."

Cooper limped forward. "Sounds like we've got some time to kill then. Why don't we head inside? I could use a cold drink after all this excitement."

Clayton's eyes lit up at the suggestion. "I wouldn't say no to some of that sweet tea of yours, Cooper. It's been a long day."

"Nothing stronger?" asked Viper.

"Nah, I have to fly the chopper home." Clayton looked nostalgic. "Gotta thank you for that. I don't get many hours behind the rotors these days. Just enough to stay qualified."

As they made their way toward the ranch house, Kat found herself walking beside Mike. Their shoulders brushed, and familiar warmth spread through her chest. She glanced up at him, noticing the way his eyes crinkled at the corners as he smiled down at her.

Clayton's voice broke through their moment. "You two look cozy again. Should I be planning to attend a re-wedding?"

Her cheeks heated, but she didn't move away from Mike. Instead, she met Clayton's gaze squarely. "We're working on it, Clayton. One step at a time."

Mike slipped his arm around her waist, pulling her closer. "That's right. We've got a lot of lost time to make up for."

As they entered the cool interior of the ranch house, Nina greeted them in the kitchen, her face etched with worry. "Is it over? Are we safe?"

Cooper wrapped his arms around her, pressing a kiss to her forehead. "For now, darlin'. We've got some breathing room."

Kat moved to help Nina and Kinsey with the drinks, pulling glasses from the cupboard as Sage retrieved a pitcher of sweet tea from the refrigerator. The domesticity of the moment struck her, a total contrast to the violence they'd just experienced.

As they settled around the large kitchen table, Clayton leaned back in his chair. "So, what's next for you all? I can't imagine you'll be content to just sit back and relax after all this."

Mike chuckled, shaking his head. "You know us better than that, Clayton. We've got some unfinished business to take care of."

Kat nodded in agreement. "The cartel might be backing off for now, but they're still out there. We can't just ignore that."

Viper, who had been quiet until now, spoke up. "We've got some contacts south of the border. Might be time to pay them a visit and see what intel we can gather."

Clayton raised an eyebrow. "You planning on taking on the entire cartel yourselves? That's a tall order, even for you guys."

Cooper leaned forward, his expression serious. "We're not looking to start a war, Clayton, but we need to make sure they understand that coming after us or our families is off-limits."

Kat found herself nodding along with Cooper's words. The thought of the cartel threatening their newfound peace made her blood boil. She caught Mike's eye across the table, seeing the same feelings reflected there.

"Whatever you decide," said Clayton, his tone cautious, "Just remember that you're not officially sanctioned for any of this. If you get caught, I can't help you."

Sawyer grinned, the cut on his forehead giving him a roguish appearance. "When have we ever needed official sanction, Clayton? We'll do what needs to be done, same as always."

The conversation drifted to lighter topics as they finished their tea, but she could sense the undercurrent of nervous anticipation running through the group.

A while later, Clayton's exfil team arrived to take custody of the prisoners. Kat watched from the porch as the cartel members were loaded into armored vehicles, faces defiant but body language defeated.

Mike joined her, slipping his arm around her waist once more. "Penny for your thoughts?"

She leaned into him, savoring his warmth. "Just thinking about how much has changed. A few days ago, I was flying cargo runs and trying to forget about all of this. Now..."

"Maybe we're safe again."

"Maybe." She leaned against him. "Hopefully."

Chapter 8—Kat

A COMFORTABLE SILENCE settled between them, filled with unspoken words and lingering glances. Kat's fingers twitched, longing to reach out and touch him. "Mike, I—" she started, her voice catching in her throat.

He raised an eyebrow, waiting for her to continue.

Kat took a deep breath, fortifying herself. "I can't keep pretending anymore. These past few days, fighting side by side with you, it's made me realize something."

Mike's brow furrowed. "What's that?"

"I love you," she blurted out, her cheeks flushing. "I always have, even after everything that happened between us. I tried to move on, to forget, but I couldn't. You're a part of me, Mike."

Mike's eyes widened, surprise and longing flashing across his face. He took a step closer to her. "Kat, I—" He paused, struggling to find the right words. "I pushed you away because I thought I was protecting you. After Afghanistan, I was a mess. The nightmares, the pain... I didn't want to drag you down with me."

She cupped Mike's face in her hands. "You should have let me decide that for myself. I would have stood by you through anything."

He leaned into her touch, his eyes closing briefly. "I know that now. God, Kat, I've missed you so much."

Without another word, he pulled Kat into his arms, crushing his lips against hers. The kiss was desperate and hungry, years of pent-up longing pouring out between them. She tangled her fingers in his hair as she pressed herself closer to him, relishing the feeling of his strong body against hers.

When they finally broke apart, both breathing heavily, Mike rested his forehead against Kat's. "I love you too, Kat. I never stopped."

Kat smiled, her heart soaring. "Then let's not waste any more time."

She took Mike's hand, leading him toward the room she'd been using. When they reached the guest room, she pulled Mike inside and locked the door behind them.

In the soft moonlight streaming through the window, Kat could see the desire burning in Mike's eyes. He reached for her, skimming his hands down her sides before coming to rest on her hips.

"Are you sure about this?" Mike asked, his voice husky.

Kat nodded, her fingers working at the buttons of his shirt. "I've never been surer of anything in my life."

Mike's shirt fell to the floor, revealing his muscular chest and the scars that told the story of his service. Kat traced them gently with her fingertips, leaning in to press soft kisses along his collarbone.

A low groan escaped Mike's lips as he pulled her closer, sliding his hands under her tank top. "God, I've missed touching you."

Kat shivered as his calloused fingers brushed against her bare skin. She tugged at the hem of her shirt, pulling it over her head and tossing it aside. He watched, looking pleased, as she revealed her body to him. "I've changed some in five years."

"No. Still the same luscious brown skin, beautiful breasts..." He trailed his fingers down her abdomen. "Flat stomach. You're as perfect as I remember."

"I'm glad you think so."

"Oh, I do."

"Good." She kissed him again, her tongue slipping between his lips. She had missed this so much. The way he tasted, the way he smelled, the way he felt, and the way he made her feel.

Mike broke the kiss, trailing his lips down her neck. "I want to taste every inch of you."

"Yes. Please."

His hands moved to her waist, unbuttoning her jeans and pushing them down her hips. She stepped out of them, kicking them aside. He cupped her ass, squeezing gently before hooking his thumbs into the waistband of her panties. He slid them down her legs, letting them fall to the floor. She was completely naked now, her body exposed to his hungry gaze.

"You're so beautiful," he murmured, running his hands over her curves. "I can't believe I almost lost you."

"You did lose me for too long." She was sad as she said it.

He winced, closing his eyes for a second. "Yeah. I wanted to protect you, but all I did was hurt you in a different way."

She touched his chest. "We were both hurt, but we can move past that. You saved me from those traffickers, and we're in different places now."

"I know. I just wish I'd done it differently."

"I understand why you didn't. I forgive you." She kissed him again, trying to convey her feelings through the kiss.

He returned the kiss, deepening it as his tongue explored her mouth. She moaned softly, pressing her body against his. She could feel his cock growing hard through his pants, and she rubbed herself against it, wanting to feel more of him. "You're wearing too many damned clothes," she said as she started tugging at his T-shirt.

"Yes, ma'am, I am." He assisted, and soon, he was naked before her.

She paused to stare at the scars on his side and hip, extending down past his knee. "You never let me really look at them before, after you came home."

"I was ashamed of them. I still am."

"They're part of you, and I love every part of you. They show how strong you are." Kat ran her fingers over the raised flesh, tracing the lines of the scars.

He shuddered, goosebumps rising on his skin. "That feels good."

"I want to make you feel good." She kissed the scar on his hip, then worked her way up to his chest. She flicked her tongue over his nipple, making him gasp.

"Fuck, that's nice."

She smiled, continuing to tease his nipples with her tongue and teeth. She loved the way he reacted to her touch, making her feel powerful and sexy. She kissed her way up to his neck, nibbling on his earlobe. "I want you inside me," she whispered.

"I want that, too." He picked her up, carrying her to the bed. He laid her down, kissing her deeply before moving to her breasts. He sucked on her nipples, making her moan with pleasure.

"Oh, yes."

"I want to taste you." He kissed her stomach, working his way down to her pussy. She spread her legs, giving him access. He pressed teasing kisses to her thighs before licking up one and down the other, passing over her mound.

"What are you doing?"

"Driving you crazy," he said without any clear sign of being sorry. "Remember how we used to make love all night?"

"I do."

"I want to take my time with you. I want to savor every moment."

"I want that, too." She moaned as he licked her clit, sending shivers of pleasure through her body.

"You taste so good." He continued to lick and suck her clit, making her writhe with pleasure. She grabbed his head, pulling him closer.

"Don't stop." Her breath was coming in short gasps as he worked her clit with his tongue. Every nerve in her body was on fire, and she strained closer, bucking against his mouth.

"I'm not stopping until you come for me." He slipped two fingers inside her, curling them just right to make her see stars.

"Oh, wow," she cried out as she came, shuddering with release. Stars exploded behind her eyes as her orgasm washed over her. The intensity was almost too much to bear, but she rode it out, clinging to him as she came down from her high.

"I missed that," he said with satisfaction. "I missed your taste and seeing how beautiful you come."

"I missed you. I missed us." She blinked her eyes. "I missed all the good times and even the bad ones. You forgetting to put down the toilet seat."

"You leaving the cap off the toothpaste."

"I did that?"

"Yeah, you did."

She laughed. "I guess we're both guilty of some things."

"I think we can agree that we've both made mistakes, but we're here now. We have a second chance to get it right. I don't want to waste another minute."

"Me neither." She pulled him close, kissing him with renewed passion. His cock was hard and ready, pressing against her thigh. She reached down, stroking him with her hand. "I need you." She guided him to her entrance, and he hovered at her entrance. "Is something wrong?"

"I don't want to hurt you if it's been a while..." He sounded unsure.

She rolled her eyes but indulgently. "If you want to know if I've been with anyone else in the past few years, the answer is no. I still felt married to you in my heart."

He looked relieved and kissed her again before easing back to say, "It was the same for me. I didn't want to let anyone get too close, and the thought of touching someone besides you..." He trailed off with a grimace. "Impossible."

She smiled, feeling a rush of relief and happiness. "Then what are you waiting for? Make love to me."

"With pleasure." He slid inside her, and they both moaned at the sensation. It was as if no time had passed, and they were picking up where they'd left off. They moved together in perfect sync, their bodies remembering each other as if no time had passed.

"You feel so good." She arched her back, pushing against him. "Just like I remember."

"So do you." He kissed her neck, making her shiver. "Better than I remember."

They moved together, finding their rhythm again. The pleasure built between them, and he thrust harder and faster. She clung to him, digging her nails into his back. She clenched her thighs around his waist, pressing her feet into the back of his thighs to keep him from getting too far away.

He groaned, burying his face in her neck. "I'm close."

"Me too." She was teetering on the edge, and it would only take a little more to send her over.

"Come with me." He reached between them, finding her clit. He rubbed it in tight circles, sending her spiraling over the edge.

"Mike," she cried out, her body trembling with release as an orgasm ripped through her. She clung to him, pussy contracting around his cock as she rode the waves of pleasure.

"I love you." He thrust once more, then stilled, spilling himself inside her.

"I love you too." She held him close, not wanting to let go.

"I never stopped loving you."

"I know." She kissed him, pouring all her feelings into the kiss. As they lay together, bodies entwined and hearts racing, she had never felt more alive. She was home, in Mike's arms, and nothing else mattered.

"I never want to let you go," he said, his lips pressed against her forehead.

"You never have to," she said, her voice filled with love and certainty. "I'm yours, Mike. Always and forever."

"I'm sorry I ever let you go," he whispered.

Kat snuggled closer, her fingers tracing lazy patterns on his chest. "We're together now. That's all that matters."

As they drifted off to sleep, wrapped in each other's arms, Kat knew that whatever challenges they faced in the future, they would face them together. The past was behind them, and a new chapter of their love story was just beginning.

Chapter 9—Kat

KAT GRIPPED THE STEERING wheel of the rental car tightly as they crossed the border into Tijuana. The bustling streets and vibrant colors of the city contrasted sharply with the tension in the vehicle. Mike sat beside her, scanning their surroundings constantly. In the backseat, Cooper and Sawyer maintained a vigilant watch.

"Clayton's intel better be solid," she muttered, navigating through the crowded streets. "We're taking a hell of a risk coming here."

Mike reached over, placing a reassuring hand on her thigh. "We've got this, Kat. The brotherhood has your back."

She nodded, grateful for his steady presence. As they approached their destination, a nondescript bar in a less touristy part of town, her heart rate quickened. This was it—the moment they'd face Javier, the rumored head of the cartel.

She parked the car a block away, and they exited cautiously. The humid air clung to her skin as they walked toward the bar, and she was tense. The faint sound of mariachi music drifted from inside as they pushed open the heavy wooden door.

The interior was dimly lit with smoke hanging in the air that made her cough. A handful of patrons nursed drinks at the bar, while others huddled in booths along the walls. Kat's gaze immediately locked onto a man sitting alone at a corner table, his presence commanding attention even in the shadows.

"That's got to be him," she whispered to Mike.

He nodded almost imperceptibly. "Let's do this."

They approached the table, Kat in the lead, with Mike at her side. Cooper and Sawyer hung back, positioning themselves strategically around the room.

"Javier?" asked Kat, her voice steady despite her racing pulse.

The man looked up, his dark eyes assessing them coolly. "Who's asking?"

She slid into the seat across from him with Mike standing protectively at her shoulder. "My name is Kat Deacon. We need to talk about Los Coyotes."

Javier's eyebrow arched slightly, the only indication of his surprise. "Bold move, coming here uninvited, *morenita*. What makes you think I have anything to do with them?"

Kat leaned forward slightly. "Because you're the one calling the shots in Tijuana. We're here to make sure the cartel understands that we're not a threat—as long as they leave us alone."

A tense silence stretched between them. Kat was grateful for Mike's presence behind her, solid and reassuring.

Finally, Javier chuckled, the sound both amused and dangerous. "You've got *cojones*, I'll give you that," he said, signaling to the bartender. "But what makes you think I won't just have you killed right here?"

She dared not look away. "Because you're smarter than that. You know eliminating us would bring more heat than it's worth. We're not here for revenge or territory. We just want to be left in peace."

He studied her for a long moment, then nodded to the bartender, who approached with a bottle of mezcal and glasses. "Tell me more about this peace you seek."

Kat relaxed slightly, sensing a shift in the conversation. "Los Coyotes and some low-level cartel members are either dead or facing prison time in the States. We're content with that outcome. We have no interest in your operations or territory. We simply want assurance that the cartel won't keep coming for us."

Javier poured three glasses of mezcal, sliding one toward Kat and one toward Mike. He raised his own glass, a wry smile playing on his lips. "You know, I've never heard of Los Coyotes, but I admire your bravery, crazy *morenita*. You're in luck—I have no quarrel with you or your friends."

Kat's eyes widened slightly at his admission. She glanced at Mike, who nodded almost imperceptibly.

"To new understandings," said Javier, raising his glass.

Kat lifted hers, the smoky aroma of the mezcal filling her nostrils. "To peace," she said.

They clinked glasses and drank. The mezcal burned pleasantly down Kat's throat, warming her from the inside.

He set his glass down, his expression turning serious. "Consider this a one-time courtesy because I think I like you. You have *agallas*. You and your people stay out of our business, and we'll stay out of yours. Agreed?"

Kat nodded solemnly. "Agreed."

A genuine smile spread across Javier's face. "Excellent. Let's enjoy this fine mezcal. Bartender, put their order on my tab." He gestured to Sawyer and Cooper. "Your friends might as well join us. They stick out in this place."

As the tension in the room dissipated, she allowed herself to relax slightly as the others joined them. She caught Mike's eye, seeing the pride and relief reflected there. They'd done it—they'd secured their safety without bloodshed.

Cooper and Sawyer approached the table, joining them for a drink. As they sat there, sipping mezcal and engaging in cautious small talk with Javier, Kat marveled at the strange turn of events. Here they were, sharing drinks with a cartel boss, having just negotiated a truce that could change their lives.

The smoky flavor of the mezcal lingered on her tongue as she listened to the men swap stories, each carefully avoiding any mention of their respective organizations. The clink of glasses, and the low hum of conversation in the bar created a surreal backdrop to their unlikely gathering.

As the night wore on, she surreptitiously studied Javier. Despite his dangerous reputation, there was an undeniable charisma about him. She could see how he'd risen to power in the ruthless world of the cartels.

"So, Kat," said Javier, refilling her glass for the fourth time, "Tell me, what does a brave *morenita* like you do when she's not negotiating with cartel bosses?"

Kat laughed, the mezcal having loosened her up slightly. "I'm a pilot, actually. I fly a small charter plane. Or I will again once the insurance check comes in."

Javier's eyes lit up with interest. "Ah, a woman of the skies. No wonder you have such a fearless spirit."

Mike tensed beside her, but she placed a calming hand on his arm. "It's a challenging job, but I love the freedom of it."

"Freedom," Javier mused, swirling the mezcal in his glass. "A precious thing, no? In my line of work, true freedom is rare."

For a moment, she glimpsed the man behind the cartel boss—someone who understood the weight of power and responsibility. She nodded, raising her glass. "To freedom, then. In whatever form we can find it."

Javier clinked his glass against hers, a look of respect in his eyes. "You're an interesting woman, Kat Deacon. I'm glad we were able to come to an understanding."

As the night drew to a close, she stood, feeling slightly unsteady from the mezcal. Mike's hand at her elbow steadied her. "Thank you for your hospitality, Javier," she said. "And for hearing us out."

Javier rose as well, inclining his head. "Safe travels, my friends. Remember our agreement, and you'll have nothing to fear from me or mine."

They made their way out of the bar, the cool night air a relief after the smoky interior. As they walked back to their car, Kat leaned into Mike, feeling the adrenaline of the evening finally start to ebb.

"We did it," she murmured.

Mike wrapped an arm around her waist, pulling her close. "You did it, Kat. That was all you in there. He wanted you." He sounded jealous.

She smiled up at him, feeling a surge of affection. "Maybe, but he must have realized I'm taken. And I couldn't have done it without you guys backing me up."

As they reached the car, Cooper clapped her on the shoulder. "Damn fine job, Kat. You've got balls of steel."

Sawyer nodded in agreement. "Never thought I'd be sharing drinks with a cartel boss, but you pulled it off."

Cooper hadn't been drinking as much, so he took over driving, since she was in no state. As they drove away from the bar, a weight lifted. They'd faced down one of their greatest fears and come out on top. Kat allowed herself a small smile. They'd done the impossible tonight and lived to tell the tale. Whatever the future held, she knew she could handle it—with Mike and the Brotherhood by her side.

COOPER GUIDED THE RENTAL car through the neon-lit streets of Tijuana while she watched, scanning for a suitable hotel. The adrenaline from their meeting with Javier still coursed through her veins, making her hyper-aware of every shadow and movement around them.

"There." Mike pointed to a well-lit establishment with a clean facade. "Looks decent enough."

Kat nodded, and Cooper pulled into the parking lot. The hotel stood out among its neighbors, its freshly painted exterior and manicured landscaping a jarring difference to the grittier surroundings. As they stepped out of the car, the warm night air enveloped them, carrying the faint scent of street food and exhaust.

The four of them entered, finding the interior was surprisingly upscale, with polished marble floors and tasteful artwork adorning the walls. Kat's boots clicked against the tile as she approached the front desk alongside Mike, following Cooper and Sawyer, who each secured their own rooms first. The clerk, a young man with a friendly smile, greeted them in accented English.

"Welcome to 'Hotel Paseo.' How may I assist you this evening?"

Mike handled the transaction while Kat surveyed the lobby. Despite the late hour, a few other guests milled about, their quiet conversations creating a low hum in the background.

"Room four-twelve," said Mike, turning to her with the key card. "Fourth floor, corner suite."

They made their way to the elevator, the tension in Kat's shoulders easing slightly as the doors closed behind them. As they ascended, she leaned against Mike, drawing comfort from his solid presence.

Sawyer and Cooper got off on the second floor, having rooms across from each other. Then it was just her and Mike. "I can't believe we did that," she said, still in disbelief at the outcome of their meeting with Javier.

Mike wrapped an arm around her waist, pulling her close. "Yeah. You're a crazy *morenita*, and I'm the foolish *gringo* who will follow you anywhere."

The elevator dinged, and they stepped out into a carpeted hallway. Their room was at the end, offering a view of the city skyline. As Mike swiped the key card, a moment of weakness plagued her. The enormity of what they'd accomplished tonight finally hit her.

The suite was spacious and tastefully decorated, with a king-sized bed dominating the main room. Floor-to-ceiling windows offered a panoramic view of Tijuana's twinkling lights. Kat moved to the window, pressing her palm against the cool glass as she gazed out at the city.

"It's beautiful," she said softly. "Hard to believe what's lurking beneath the surface."

Mike joined her at the window, his reflection visible in the glass. "That's true of most places, and people."

Kat turned to face him, struck by the intensity in his eyes. Without warning, Mike cupped her face in his hands and kissed her deeply. Kat responded instantly, her body molding against his as years of pent-up longing and desire flooded through her.

They stumbled toward the bed, hands fumbling with buttons and zippers. Kat's shirt hit the floor, followed quickly by Mike's. As they fell onto the mattress, Kat reveled in the feeling of Mike's skin against hers, his muscular body pressing her into the soft sheets.

Mike trailed kisses down her neck, his stubble scraping deliciously against her sensitive skin. Kat arched into him, her fingers tangling in his hair as he lavished attention on her breasts. Every touch sent sparks of pleasure shooting through her body.

She gasped as his hand slipped between her thighs to stroke her pussy. "Please."

He looked up at her, his eyes dark with desire. "Tell me what you want, Kat."

"All of you."

With a growl, Mike captured her lips in another searing kiss as he entered her. Kat moaned into his mouth, wrapping her legs around his waist to pull him deeper. They moved together in a frenzied rhythm.

Her world narrowed to the sensations he was evoking in her body. The drag of his skin against hers, the weight of him above her, and the way he filled her so perfectly—it was overwhelming in the best possible way. She clung to him, digging her nails into his back as she felt herself spiraling toward the edge.

"Let go, Kat," he whispered in her ear, his voice rough with exertion. "I've got you."

His words pushed her over the precipice. She cried out as her orgasm washed over her. Mike followed soon after, burying his face in the crook of her neck as he found his release.

They lay tangled together in the aftermath, their breathing slowly returning to normal. Kat traced lazy patterns on Mike's chest, savoring the feeling of his skin beneath her fingertips. She had dreamed of this moment for so long, but the reality was far better than anything her imagination could conjure, and it would take at least two or three years of lovemaking to stamp out thoughts of their time apart.

Mike pressed a kiss to her forehead. He reached up, tucking a stray lock of hair behind her ear as his expression grew serious. "Remarry me, Kat."

Kat's breath caught in her throat. "What?"

Mike sat up, taking her hands in his. "I know it's sudden, but life's too short for regrets. I pushed you away once because I thought I was protecting you. I won't make that mistake again." He brought her hand to his lips, kissing her knuckles. "Marry me. Be my wife again, my partner in everything."

Tears welled in her eyes as she nodded, overwhelmed by emotion. "Yes," she whispered. "Yes, I'll marry you again."

Mike's face lit up with a smile brighter than the Tijuana skyline. He pulled her into his arms, kissing her deeply. As they fell back onto the bed, limbs entwined, her heart soared with joy and hope for their future together.

As they made love again, slower this time, savoring every touch and caress, Kat marveled at how quickly life could change. Just hours ago, they'd been negotiating with a cartel boss, their lives hanging in the balance. Now, they were engaged again and planning a renewed future together.

Afterward, they lay facing each other, legs tangled beneath the sheets. He traced the curve of her hip, his touch reverent. "I can't believe we wasted so much time," he said softly.

She shook her head, placing a finger on his lips. "It wasn't wasted. Everything we've been through led us here, to this moment. We're stronger for it."

He kissed her finger, then pulled her closer. "You're right, and now we have the rest of our lives to make up for lost time."

Chapter 10—Mike

THREE WEEKS LATER, Mike stood at the makeshift altar nestled between two towering oak trees on Cooper's ranch. He was surrounded by this gathering of friends and family, but his focus was on the aisle as his heart raced while he waited impatiently for Kat to appear.

The soft strains of violin music filled the air, and he held his breath as Kat emerged from the farmhouse. She wore a simple white sundress that flowed around her curves and accentuated her dark skin. Her natural hair was adorned with delicate wildflowers instead of a veil. As she walked down the aisle, she looked at him, and a radiant smile lit up her face.

His hands trembled slightly as he took Kat's hands in his when she reached him. Cooper, standing beside them as the best man, cleared his throat and the officiant began the ceremony.

"We're gathered here today to witness the union of Mike Deacon and Katriona 'Kat' Collins," said the judge they'd hired for the job, his gruff voice softened by emotion. "These two have faced more challenges than most couples ever will, but they've come out stronger for it."

Mike squeezed Kat's hands, remembering the long road that had brought them to this moment. The pain of pushing her away after his injuries, the years of separation, and the danger that had reunited them—it all seemed to fade away as he gazed into her eyes.

Judge Wu continued, "Mike and Kat, you are here to enter the solemn state of matrimony—"

"Again," heckled Viper from the crowd.

The judge didn't blink when Mike made a rude hand gesture to his friend. He continued on as if nothing had happened, finally reaching the point where it was time to trade rings. Once it was on his finger, Mike marveled at the simple gold band that now adorned his finger. It was the one he'd worn for years and then tucked away in a box the day the divorce was finalized. Kat had retained hers as well, and they'd decided to use their old rings as the cornerstone of rebuilding their new life together. It was good to have it back where it belonged.

Judge Wu said, "By the power vested in me by the great state of Texas, I now pronounce you husband and wife. Mike, you may kiss your bride."

Mike cupped Kat's face in his hands, drawing her close for a tender kiss. The assembled crowd erupted in cheers and applause, their joy echoing across the ranch.

As they turned to face their friends and family, Mike's looked out over the gathering. Sawyer and Kinsey stood arm in arm, their faces beaming with happiness. Viper and Sage shared a knowing look, their own love story still unfolding. Nina leaned against Cooper, wiping away a tear as Caleb grinned up at them.

The reception was a lively affair, with tables set up under strings of twinkling lights. The scent of barbecue wafted through the air as Cooper manned the grill, flipping steaks with practiced ease. Laughter and conversation flowed freely as the extended family celebrated together.

When it was time for the first dance, Mike led Kat to the makeshift dance floor, pulling her close as the first notes of their song played. As they swayed together, he whispered in her ear, "I can't believe we're finally here."

Kat smiled up at him, her eyes shining. "Believe it, Mr. Deacon. You're stuck with me now."

He chuckled, spinning her out and then drawing her back into his arms. "There's nowhere else I'd rather be, Mrs. Deacon."

As the night wore on, Mike found himself sitting at a table with Cooper, Sawyer, and Viper. The four men clinked their beer bottles together in a toast.

"To Mike and Kat," said Sawyer, grinning. "It's about damn time you two got your act together."

Mike laughed, shaking his head. "Yeah, yeah. I was an idiot for letting her go in the first place."

Cooper leaned back in his chair, his expression thoughtful. "We've all made mistakes, brother. The important thing is that you found your way back to each other."

Viper nodded in agreement. "And now she's part of this crazy family for good. No takebacks."

As they teased and heckled him a bit more, he just grinned. These men were more than just friends or comrades—they were his brothers in every sense of the word.

Kat joined them, perching on Mike's lap and stealing a sip of his beer. "What are you boys gossiping about over here?"

He wrapped an arm around her waist, pulling her closer. "Just reliving some of our glory days. Did I ever tell you about the time Viper here tried to sweet-talk his way past a checkpoint using nothing but bad Pashto and worse dance moves?"

Viper groaned, covering his face with his hand. "I thought we agreed never to speak of that again."

Kat laughed. "Oh, now this I have to hear. Spill it, boys."

As the story unfolded, with each man adding his own embellishments and commentary, Mike found himself overcome with gratitude. Not just for Kat and the love they shared, but for this entire makeshift family that had come together against all odds. They'd slowly gathered around, and now, they formed a half-circle, listening to the silly story. It was a perfect moment.

Later, as the party began to wind down, Mike and Kat stood on the porch of the farmhouse, looking out over the sprawling Texas landscape. The stars twinkled brightly in the clear night sky, and a cool breeze rustled through the trees.

Mike wrapped his arms around Kat from behind, resting his chin on her shoulder. "So, Mrs. Deacon, are you ready for our next adventure?"

Kat leaned back against him, sighing contentedly. "As long as I'm with you, I'm ready for anything."

He turned her in his arms, gazing into her eyes. "I love you, Kat. More than anything."

She reached up, tracing the line of his jaw with her fingertips. "I love you too, Mike. Always have and always will."

As they shared a tender kiss, the sounds of laughter and music drifted from the reception. It was a reminder of the family they had built. He broke the kiss, resting his forehead against hers. "You know, I never thought I'd have this again. A family, a home, and a purpose beyond just surviving."

Kat nodded, understanding in her eyes. "I know what you mean. After everything we've been through, it almost feels too good to be true."

He shook his head, a smile tugging at his lips. "No, it's real. We've earned this happiness, Kat, and I intend to cherish every moment of it."

As they turned back to rejoin the celebration, Mike felt a sense of anticipation for the future. The night air was filled with the promise of new beginnings, of love that had weathered storms and come out stronger, and as he looked around at the faces of those he held dear, he knew that this was just the start of a new chapter in their lives—one filled with hope, love, and the unbreakable bonds of family.

Epilogue—Kat

KAT SHIFTED AWKWARDLY on the couch, her swollen belly making it difficult to find a comfortable position. The Texas sun streamed through the windows of their own ranch house, which included a hanger and a private airstrip. Her plane was grounded in the hanger for the moment, since she was on maternity leave, but knowing it awaited made her happy. To her surprise, the repair crew had been able to save her old Pilatus, so she could keep flying her dad's plane for a while longer—once she was back in the skies in a few months.

She glanced at the clock for what felt like the hundredth time that morning. Mike had only been gone for fifteen minutes to check on the horses, but his absence left her feeling antsy.

"I swear, if this baby doesn't come soon, I'm going to lose my mind," she muttered to herself, rubbing her lower back.

The sound of boots on the porch had her perking up. Mike entered, breaking into a wide smile at the sight of her.

"How're you feeling, sweetheart?" He crossed the room in a few long strides, kneeling beside her.

Kat rolled her eyes. "The same as I was fifteen minutes ago when you asked before leaving."

Mike chuckled, placing a gentle hand on her belly. "Just checking. You know I worry."

"You don't say," said Kat dryly, but she couldn't force back a smile. Mike's constant hovering over the past few weeks had been driving her crazy, but deep down, she loved how attentive he'd become. It was a far cry from the broken man she'd divorced years ago, consumed by his PTSD and pushing her away at every turn.

"Have you eaten?" he asked, already moving toward the kitchen.

Kat sighed. "Yes, Mike. I had breakfast an hour ago. You were there, remember?"

He paused, looking sheepish. "Right. Sorry. I just want to make sure you're taken care of."

"I know," said Kat softly. "And I appreciate it, but I'm not an invalid. I can still do things for myself."

Mike nodded, returning to her side. "You're right. I'll try to dial it back a notch."

Kat reached out, taking his hand. "I do love you for it, you know. Even if I complain."

His eyes softened, and he leaned in to press a kiss to her forehead. "I love you too. Both of you."

As he pulled away, a sharp pain rippled across her abdomen. She gasped, tightening her grip on Mike's hand.

"Kat?" Mike's voice was laced with concern. "What is it?"

She took a deep breath as the pain subsided. "I think... I think that was a contraction."

Mike's eyes widened. "Are you sure? Should we call the doctor?"

Kat shook her head. "Not yet. It could be false labor. Let's wait and see if I have another one."

The next twenty minutes passed in tense silence, Mike hovering nearby. When the second contraction hit, stronger than the first, Kat knew this was it.

"Okay," she said, her voice steadier than she felt. "It's time to go to the hospital."

He sprang into action, grabbing the pre-packed hospital bag and helping Kat to her feet. As they made their way to the truck, she paused, another contraction washing over her.

"You okay?" Mike asked, his arm supporting her.

Kat nodded, breathing through the pain. "Yeah. Just...promise me something?"

"Anything," he said without hesitation.

"Don't let go of my hand," she said, looking up at him. "No matter what happens in that delivery room, don't let go."

Mike's eyes shone with emotion. "Never. I'm not going anywhere."

The drive to the hospital was a blur of contractions and Mike's soothing voice, reminding Kat to breathe. By the time they arrived, which took almost an hour due to their remote location, her contractions were coming faster and stronger.

As they wheeled Kat into the delivery room, she gripped Mike's hand tightly. "I'm scared," she said softly.

Mike leaned down, pressing his forehead to hers. "You've got this, Kat. I'll be right here with you, every step of the way."

Hours passed in a haze of pain and determination. She pushed with everything she had, Mike's steady presence beside her giving her strength. Finally, with one last monumental effort, their son entered the world with a loud, healthy cry.

"It's a boy," said the doctor, placing the squirming infant on Kat's chest.

Kat stared down at their son in awe, tears streaming down her face. "He's perfect," she whispered. He was a beautiful blend of the two of them, with light-brown skin and big, dark eyes, along with a few sparse wisps of brown hair that looked to wave but not fully curl.

Mike's arm wrapped around her shoulders, his own eyes wet with tears. "He's beautiful. Just like his mother."

As the nurses cleaned and measured the baby, she turned to her husband. "Thank you," she said, her voice thick with emotion. "For him...and for us."

He kissed her cheek. "Thank you for giving me a second chance and believing in me when I couldn't believe in myself."

The nurse returned, placing their swaddled son in Kat's arms. As they gazed down at their newborn, rightness washed over her. This was what they had fought for, what they had overcome so much to achieve.

"What should we name him?" he asked softly, stroking the baby's cheek with a gentle finger. "I know we said we'd have a name for him when we saw him, and I have one in mind."

Kat smiled. "Me too. Say it together?"

He nodded, lifting three fingers. When the last one went down, she said, "Joel."

At the same time, Mike said, "Joel." He grinned. "After your father."

"He'd have been so happy." She blinked back tears, feeling happy and a little melancholy that her father wouldn't be part of this moment or any others in the future. They'd have to ensure they told the baby so much about him that he'd feel like he knew his grandfather.

As little Joel yawned and winked up at them, she leaned into Mike's embrace. They had come so far, overcome so much, and now, with their son in their arms, she couldn't imagine anything but a happy future ahead of them.

Get The Whole Series:[1]

About Mia

THANK YOU FOR READING! I hope you enjoyed reading this book as much as I loved writing it!

If so, you might be interested in my reader club, where you'll get notice of new releases, specials, and other great goodies (like FREE books and FREE Chapters of upcoming releases).

As a special thank you, **you'll immediately get my book The Boardroom Connection, for FREE when you sign up**. No strings, you can unsubscribe anytime, and I promise I won't blow up your inbox.

What do you think?

<u>YES—I'm in! I want to know the moment you drop a new release and get my FREE book!</u>[1]

No, that's alright. I get enough emails, and I'll keep up with your new releases another way.

Again, I hope you enjoyed this book. You can learn more about my newest releases here: https://bwwmlovestories.com/latest-releases/mia-latest/[2]

---

1. **https://dl.bookfunnel.com/g14g65dcmd**

2. https://l.facebook.com/l.php?u=https%3A%2F%2Fbwwmlovestories.com%2Flatest-releases%2Fmia-latest%2F%3Ffbclid%3DIwZXh0bgNhZW0CMTAAAR34HFLR7qBe4ZmBHns_e4d0XgNzeLpuTKitrQtc8gfqYam6Jwke4d05P5M_aem_AXZgxaooVqdkRI8v5k6ceTy7Gin_SGSOwZ0mohUpkMmzR-Suzibzrob5LkW28qL53CXma0uvn_jG_N2FBJWICaiR&h=AT0CMUeqAaRQCxB-vibJCLOB3BJo5qSFoE64VilifGretJ6ZtzkQOn3BhZ4e4cTX1Dpuw0RpYrElXkhsQlqHZNi1DZdWlWOBOS2jn6YcuV5YinE0EhazJOy56rM3zQC4ziRiIOHCHTe8ohj45g&__tn__=-

And if you get a chance to drop a review or rating, I'd really appreciate it.

Best,

Mia

UK-

R&c%5b0%5d=AT06pfvEYO5wdSYGkilnE_RlU_XJQ3YtaKVXM3kw2RVJU7AEHMWZr

Kbz4ZVZ5KpHSvCa7Rpb3D9k4_NQuxDrhwHZHAVAvzrcdwCUjfoVuAu6L2M3OoNNZ

9qa849xyadSBygYxrAoFCijWjBix80lUGrim2l7h4DWuGnd8vRM3D-hcJAbp-

sg41WLy5X32P7Q

About Mylia

IF YOU WOULD LIKE TO be the first to hear about new releases, please join my mailing list[1] and receive a free book. I love to hear from readers, so please feel free to email me at myliaashton@authorcooperative.com.

---

1. https://subscribeto.eo.page/myliaashton

Also by Mia Caldwell

The Brotherhood
Saved By The Master Sergeant
Sheltered By The Sergeant Major
Shielded By The Staff Sergeant
Safeguarded By The First Sergeant

Standalone
Marooned With The Billionaire Doctor
Enemies To Expecting
Ennemis En Attente
Feinde zu Erwartende

Also by Mylia Ashton

The Brotherhood
Saved By The Master Sergeant
Sheltered By The Sergeant Major
Shielded By The Staff Sergeant
Safeguarded By The First Sergeant

Standalone
Vegas Mistake
Marooned With The Billionaire Doctor
Enemies To Expecting
Cynthia And The Prince
Desperate Measures
Inferno